The Ghost of Shantel Thompson

Curtis Maynard

Maynard Productions

"For the ones that have moved on from this world before the time alloted them, those spirits feed on unfinished business and only seek rest when that business is finished."
-UNKOWN PARANORMAL INVESTIGATOR

Prologue

The sun cast a warm golden glow through the windows of the new house as the family of four eagerly unloaded boxes from the moving truck. Charlotte, a bright-eyed nine-year-old girl with curly brown hair, skipped around the empty rooms, her excitement palpable. Alvin, her five-year-old brother with a mischievous grin, trailed behind her, clutching a stuffed dinosaur tightly in his small hands.

Olivia, their mother, surveyed the spacious living room, envisioning the memories that would soon fill the space. "Isn't this place amazing, kids?" she exclaimed, her voice filled with enthusiasm. "We're going to make so many happy memories here!"

Alvin's eyes widened with wonder as he spun around, taking in the high ceilings and the polished wooden floors. "Yeah, Mama! Will we have a big backyard to play in too?"

Olivia smiled and ruffled his hair. "Yes, sweetie, a big backyard with swings and a sandbox, just for you and Charlotte."

Charlotte, who had been exploring the house, suddenly appeared at the doorway, her eyes sparkling with excitement. "Mama, I found the perfect room for my dolls! Can we set it up now?"

Olivia chuckled and nodded. "Of course,

sweetheart. Let's start making this place feel like home."

As they began to unpack and settle in, the atmosphere was filled with anticipation and joy. The rooms slowly transformed from empty spaces to cozy havens, each reflecting the personality of its new occupant. Charlotte meticulously arranged her dolls on a shelf in her room, while Alvin happily scattered his toy cars across the floor, lost in his own little world.

The house itself seemed to radiate a sense of warmth and comfort, its walls echoing with laughter and the promise of a bright future. Little did the family know that beneath the surface, a dark secret lay dormant, waiting to reveal itself in the days to come.

*****

The days passed, and the new house settled into a familiar rhythm. But something peculiar began to unfold within its walls. Charlotte, once an outgoing and cheerful girl, started displaying odd behavior that caught her parents' attention.

One sunny afternoon, Olivia entered Charlotte's room, finding her daughter engaged in an animated conversation with no one in particular. "Charlotte, who are you talking to, honey?" Olivia asked, a touch of concern in her voice.

Charlotte turned towards her mother, a distant look in her eyes. "Oh, Mama, just my new friend," she replied, her voice tinged with an otherworldly quality. "She's so nice and understands me."

Olivia exchanged a puzzled glance with Alvin, who had followed her into the room. Alvin stood in the corner, clutching his stuffed dinosaur, his eyes wide with curiosity and confusion.

As days turned into weeks, the strange behavior continued. Charlotte's imaginary friend seemed to dominate her interactions, leaving her little time to engage with her brother, Alvin. Alvin, in turn, became a habitual wailer, often crying for no discernible reason. His tears flowed freely as he pointed to different angles in the house, as if seeing something that remained invisible to everyone else.

One evening, Olivia sat on the edge of Charlotte's bed, concern etched on her face. "Sweetheart, why are you spending so much time with your imaginary friend? You used to play with Alvin and have so much fun together."

Charlotte's eyes darted around the room as if searching for her unseen companion. "Alvin is just a baby, Mama. He doesn't understand. But my friend does. She listens to me."

Olivia's heart sank, a wave of unease

washing over her. She couldn't shake the feeling that something was deeply amiss in their new home. It was as if an invisible presence had cast a shadow over her children, leaving them disconnected and isolated from each other.

Alvin, sensing the tension in the room, tugged at Olivia's sleeve. Tears streamed down his chubby cheeks as he whimpered, "Mama, I don't like it here. I see scary things. Make them go away."

Olivia's heart broke as she gathered both her children in a tight embrace. "We'll figure this out, my darlings," she whispered, her voice filled with determination. "We'll find a way to make everything better. I promise."

*****

Olivia and Charles exchanged worried glances as they sat at the kitchen table after putting the children to bed. The weight of their children's strange behavior hung heavily in the air, and they knew they needed to seek help from someone with expertise in dealing with such matters.

"I can't bear to see Charlotte and Alvin like this," Olivia said, her voice trembling with concern. "We need to find someone who can help us understand what's happening."

Charles nodded in agreement, his brow furrowed with worry. "I've been doing some research," he confessed. "And I came across some stories about this house. It seems there may be a dark history here."

Olivia's eyes widened with surprise. "What do you mean? What kind of history?"

Charles took a deep breath, trying to steady his nerves. "According to some of our neighbors, there was a young girl who was murdered in this house many years ago. Some believe her spirit might still linger here."

A chill ran down Olivia's spine, her mind racing with a mix of disbelief and fear. "Do you think that's what's affecting our children? Some kind of haunting?"

Charles shrugged, his face filled with uncertainty. "I don't know, but it's worth considering. We owe it to Charlotte and Alvin to explore every possible explanation."

Determined to find answers, Olivia and Charles decided to reach out to their neighbors, hoping to gather more information about the house's history and any paranormal encounters others might have had. They set out the next day, knocking on doors and engaging in conversations that sent shivers down their spines.

One neighbor, an elderly woman with a kind smile, shared a chilling tale. "I've lived here for decades," she began, her voice quivering with remembrance. "They say a young girl met a tragic end in that house. Some believe her spirit lingers, unable to find peace."

Olivia's eyes widened, her heart heavy with a mixture of sadness and apprehension. "Is there anything we can do? How can we protect our children?"

The neighbor's gaze softened, filled with empathy. "There are experts who deal with such matters, spiritual advisors or paranormal investigators. They might be able to help you understand what you're dealing with and find a way to bring peace to the house."

With newfound hope, Olivia and Charles thanked the neighbor for her insights and returned home, their minds racing with thoughts of seeking external help. They knew that time was of the essence, and they would stop at nothing to ensure the well-being of their children.

*****

Olivia and Charles sat side by side on the living room couch, surrounded by flickering candlelight, as they made phone calls to spiritual advisors and paranormal experts. Their voices were filled with a mix of desperation and hope, seeking guidance in their quest to understand and resolve the mysterious occurrences in their new home.

After several conversations, they finally found an experienced paranormal investigator who agreed to meet them in person. The investigator, a middle-aged man named Richard, arrived the following afternoon, carrying a bag filled with various equipment used to detect and communicate with supernatural entities.

As Richard stepped through the front door, he looked around the house, his eyes scanning the rooms with a trained gaze. "This place certainly has a history," he remarked, his voice laced with curiosity.

Olivia and Charles exchanged nervous glances, their hearts pounding in their chests. "Can you tell us more about what might be happening?" Olivia asked, her voice tinged with trepidation.

Richard nodded, his expression serious. "Based on the stories I've heard, there's a strong possibility that the spirit of a young girl may be present here. Sometimes, unresolved emotions or traumatic events can leave imprints on a location, causing disturbances."

Charles leaned forward, his voice barely

above a whisper. "What can we do, Richard? How can we help our children?"

Richard met their gaze with a reassuring smile. "First, we need to confirm if there is indeed a presence here. I'll conduct thorough investigations using specialized equipment and techniques. Once we have a better understanding of the situation, we can work towards finding a resolution."

Over the next few days, Richard meticulously explored every corner of the house, setting up cameras, meters, and audio recording devices. Olivia and Charles watched anxiously as he studied the collected data, hoping for answers that would bring them closer to a solution.

Finally, Richard called them into the living room, his face a mix of concern and certainty. "I have reviewed the evidence, and there is indeed paranormal activity in this house," he began. "The presence seems to be centered around your children, particularly Charlotte."

Olivia's heart sank, her protective instincts kicking into overdrive. "What can we do, Richard? We can't let this continue."

Richard nodded, his voice filled with empathy. "Based on my experience, I would recommend a cleansing ritual, a spiritual intervention to help release the trapped energy and bring peace to the house. It's important to prioritize the well-being of your children and create a safe environment for them."

Olivia and Charles exchanged a determined look, their love for their children fueling their resolve. They thanked Richard for his guidance and vowed to do whatever it took to protect their family. The path ahead was uncertain, but their determination to find a resolution grew stronger with each passing moment.

******

The air in the house felt heavy as Olivia and Charles prepared for the cleansing ritual. They had gathered candles, sage bundles, and other ceremonial tools recommended by Richard. The living room became a makeshift altar, adorned with symbols of protection and peace.

Richard stood at the center, guiding Olivia and Charles through the process. "We'll begin by creating a sacred space," he explained, his voice calm and steady. "Light the candles and let their gentle glow fill the room with positive energy."

As the flames flickered, casting dancing shadows on the walls, Richard instructed them to hold hands and close their eyes. Together, they focused their thoughts on love, protection, and the intention to release any negative energy that might be lingering.

"Imagine a warm, radiant light surrounding us," Richard continued, his voice gentle and soothing. "Feel its comforting embrace, its power to heal and cleanse."

They stood in the circle of light, the scent of sage filling the air as Richard moved around the room, wafting the smoke to purify the space. Olivia and Charles followed his lead, their minds filled with hope and determination.

"Now," Richard said, his voice carrying a sense of authority, "let us call upon the spirits of this house. Those who may be trapped or unsettled, we invite you to find peace and move on to where you truly belong."

A hush fell over the room as they waited, their hearts beating in anticipation. Then, slowly, a soft breeze rustled through the open windows, as if in response to the invocation. The atmosphere seemed to shift, as if an unseen presence stirred in acknowledgement.

Olivia's eyes filled with tears as she silently sent a message to the spirit that might be haunting their home. "We mean you no harm," she whispered. "Please find peace and allow our children to be free from any influence that may be holding them back."

Alvin, his small hand gripping Olivia's tightly, added his own plea. "We want to be happy here," he murmured. "Please, let us be happy."

The room fell into silence once more, the only sound the subtle crackling of the candles. After what felt like an eternity, Richard spoke softly, his voice filled with compassion. "I believe the ritual has had its effect. The energy feels lighter now, more serene."

Olivia and Charles looked at each other, a mix of relief and gratitude washing over them. They embraced, their bodies trembling with the weight of the experience.

******

Weeks had passed since the cleansing ritual, and Charles, Olivia, Alvin, and Charlotte began to settle into a semblance of normalcy. The house was filled with laughter and warmth once again, and they hoped that the paranormal disturbances were behind them. But their relief was short-lived.

One evening after Charles had gone on a business trip, as Olivia prepared dinner in the kitchen, she heard a series of loud crashes coming from Charlotte's room. Alvin, who was playing nearby, froze in fear, his eyes wide with alarm.

"Mama, what was that?" Alvin whispered, his voice trembling.

Olivia's heart raced as she rushed towards Charlotte's room, Alvin right on her heels. They swung open the door, only to find the room in disarray. Toys were strewn across the floor, furniture overturned, and the air crackled with an eerie energy.

"Charlotte!" Olivia called out, her voice filled with concern. "Are you okay?"

But there was no response. Charlotte was nowhere to be found. Panic gripped Olivia's chest as she frantically searched the room, her eyes darting from corner to corner.

Suddenly, a chilling gust of wind swept through the room, blowing the curtains violently and extinguishing the candles on Charlotte's nightstand. The atmosphere grew dense and suffocating, as if an unseen presence had materialized.

Alvin grabbed Olivia's hand, his grip tight and trembling. "Mama, I'm scared," he whimpered.

Olivia's motherly instincts kicked into overdrive as she scooped Alvin into her arms. "We need to find Charlotte," she said, her voice filled with determination. "We can't let her be lost in this chaos."

They made their way through the house, calling out Charlotte's name, their voices echoing in the tense silence. As they reached the staircase, a faint whisper drifted through the air, barely audible but unmistakably Charlotte's voice.

"Mama... Help me."

Olivia's heart sank, her fear mingling with a fierce sense of protectiveness. She rushed up the stairs, Alvin clinging to her tightly, and followed the sound of her daughter's plea.

They entered the attic, a dimly lit space filled with long-forgotten belongings. In the center of the room stood Charlotte, her eyes vacant and distant. She seemed entranced, oblivious to her surroundings.

"Charlotte!" Olivia called out, her voice quivering with emotion. "Snap out of it, sweetheart! It's Mama!"

But Charlotte remained unresponsive, her gaze fixed on a dusty old trunk in the corner of the attic. Olivia approached cautiously, her heart pounding in her chest.

"She needs my help! My friend needs my help but I don't understand how!" Charlotte cried as she shivered in her corner.

"Snap out of it, sweetheart!

****

The darkness in the attic seemed to press in on Olivia, Alvin, and Charlotte, filling the space with an ominous presence. Fear gripped Olivia's heart as Charlotte clutched tightly to an invisible object like it was an imaginary knife. She was seemingly not in control of her mind. Olivia could say she was almost in a complete trance. She thought about calling her husband on his phone but her own phone was in the room. She couldn't look away from Charlotte for a split second.

"Alvin, stay close," Olivia whispered, her voice trembling with a mix of determination and fear. "We need to get out of here."

Alvin nodded, his small hand gripping Olivia's tightly. Charlotte remained unresponsive, her trance-like state unbroken. With cautious steps, Olivia led them back down the attic stairs, their footsteps muffled by the weight of the unsettling silence.

As they reached the safety of the lower levels, Olivia's mind raced with thoughts of their family's well-being. The incidents had escalated beyond what they could handle, and the safety of her children took precedence over anything else.

Olivia made a firm decision. She would protect her family at all costs, even if it meant leaving their beloved home behind but unsure what Charles might think about such decision. With a heavy heart, she gathered Alvin and Charlotte in the living room, where they had once found solace and happiness.

"Listen, my loves," Olivia said, her voice filled with a mix of sadness and determination. "We're probably going to leave this house. It's not safe for us anymore. Our family's well-being comes first. I just have to convince your father to reason along"

Alvin's eyes welled up with tears, a mix of confusion and sadness evident on his face. "But Mama, I love this house," he whispered, his voice filled with a childlike innocence.

Olivia hugged him tightly, her own tears threatening to spill. "I know, my sweet boy," she replied, her voice choked with emotion. "But sometimes we have to make difficult choices to keep ourselves safe. We'll find a new home where we can make new memories, I promise."

Charlotte, still in her distant state, looked up at Olivia, seemingly aware of the weight of the decision. Olivia's heart broke for her daughter, knowing that the spirit of the young girl had latched onto Charlotte, causing her distress and endangering their lives.

Olivia's phone began to ring, breaking the silence of the night.

****

Charles's heart pounded in his chest as he dialed Olivia's number, his voice urgent with a mixture of fear and determination. He needed to convey the urgency of their situation.

As the phone rang, Charles's mind replayed the horrifying nightmare he had just experienced. The image of Charlotte, their own daughter transformed into a vengeful spirit, haunted his thoughts. He couldn't shake the feeling that their lives were in imminent danger.

Olivia picked up the phone, her voice filled with concern. "Charles, what's wrong? You sound panicked."

"Olivia, we have to leave the property immediately," Charles said, his voice trembling. "I had a nightmare, a terrible nightmare. Charlotte, or whatever has taken over her, was trying to kill us. She killed our son, and she was coming after you and me."

Olivia gasped, her hand instinctively covering her mouth. "Oh my God, Charles. Are you okay? Is this just a nightmare?"

Charles took a deep breath, trying to steady his racing heart. "I woke up, but the fear was so real," he explained. "We can't ignore this. We need to move, to protect ourselves and ensure our safety."

Olivia hesitated for a moment, the gravity of Charles's words sinking in. She knew he wouldn't make such a decision lightly. "Okay, Charles," she finally replied, her voice filled with a mix of worry and determination. "I trust your instincts. Come home, and we'll talk about it."

Charles nodded, even though Olivia couldn't see him. "I'm on my way, I can't wait for daybreak." He said, his voice resolute. "We'll figure this out together."

As Charles hung up the phone, the remnants of his nightmare still lingered in his mind. He couldn't shake the image of Charlotte's haunting gaze and the chilling sound of her voice. He knew they had to act swiftly to protect themselves and find a way to bring an end to the malevolent presence that had taken hold of their daughter.

With a sense of urgency, Charles started his car and raced back home. Thoughts raced through his mind, contemplating the best course of action to keep his family safe. He knew they couldn't stay in that house any longer, not with the threat that loomed over them.

Upon reaching home, Charles found Olivia waiting for him, her eyes filled with worry and anticipation. They embraced, seeking solace and strength in each other's arms.

Charles shared the details of his nightmare, recounting the events with a shudder. Olivia listened intently, her face etched with concern. The gravity of the situation weighed heavily on them both.

"We can't risk staying here any longer, Olivia," Charles said, his voice filled with conviction. "We have to find a new place, a safe place where we can start fresh, away from whatever force has taken over Charlotte."

Olivia nodded with understanding, her eyes filled with determination. "I agree, Charles. Our family's safety is paramount. We'll find a new home, gather our belongings, and leave this nightmare behind."

They spent the following hours making plans and reaching out to friends and family for temporary accommodation. The urgency of their situation propelled them into action, fueled by the need to protect themselves and escape the clutches of the supernatural.

As they packed their belongings, their hands moved swiftly, driven by a sense of urgency and a shared determination to leave the haunted property behind. They couldn't shake the feeling that time was running out, that they were in a race against an unseen force.

With their essentials packed, Charles and Olivia cast one last sorrowful glance at their once-beloved home. It now stood as a haunting reminder of the horrors they had endured. But they held onto hope, knowing that by leaving, they were taking a crucial step toward reclaiming their lives and finding a way to save their daughter from the darkness that consumed her.

Together, hand in hand, they walked out of the front door, leaving behind the nightmares and the echoes of their past. The road ahead was uncertain, but they were determined to find a new beginning, far away from the malevolent presence that had threatened to tear their family apart.

As they drove away, their hearts heavy with a mix of sadness and hope, they vowed to fight for their family's safety and find a way to bring Charlotte back from the depths of darkness. The journey ahead would be arduous, but their love and determination would guide them through the darkest of nights.

∞ ∞ ∞

Chapter 1

Mobile, Alabama's courtroom buzzed with anticipation as Gary and Sharon Riggs anxiously awaited the life-changing moment. The room, adorned with polished oak paneling and bathed in a warm, golden light streaming through tall windows, was steeped in an atmosphere of solemnity and hope. The air hummed with a mixture of nervous energy and quiet determination.

Seated side by side on a wooden bench, Gary and Sharon clutched each other's hands, their palms moist with perspiration. The weight of their longing and the countless hurdles they had overcome to reach this point bore heavily upon them. Mobile, known for its tranquility, had become a backdrop to their journey, a place where dreams were about to be realized.

Judge Ramirez, a figure of authority draped in a black robe, presided over the proceedings from an elevated bench. Her voice, resonating with measured authority, echoed through the room. Sharon's ears strained to catch every word, but her mind was consumed by thoughts of the child she yearned to call her own.

The judge's words seemed to stretch on, a blur of legal formalities and meticulous scrutiny. Sharon's heart pounded in her chest, her emotions tangled between impatience and a fervent desire for the judge to reach a verdict. All she wanted was to embrace their daughter, to offer her the love and security she deserved after enduring a difficult past.

"Honey, everything is going to work out. There's no reason why she would turn us down from getting the adoption," Gary's voice, soft and reassuring, broke through Sharon's restless thoughts. His words were a lifeline, a reminder that their journey was nearing its end.

"I know, but I'd feel better if she would get to the point where it's official already," Sharon sighed.

Finally, the judge's gaze shifted towards the little girl, Shantel Thompson, who sat at a table nearby. Sharon's eyes followed suit, and her heart swelled with tenderness at the sight of the child who had captured their hearts. Shantel's presence in their lives had been a beacon of hope, and they were determined to provide her with a future brighter than any she had known before.

"Mr. and Mrs. Riggs," Judge Ramirez began. "I've looked through all your papers and heard your stories and I don't think there would be a better couple to be the parents of ten-year-old Shantel. Shantel appears to have fit in with your family already. Congratulations, Mr. and

Mrs. Riggs. You are now the parents of Shantel Thompson."

Judge Ramirez's voice, laced with warmth and conviction, pierced the air. Her words cut through the tension, bringing forth a wave of relief and elation. The room erupted in applause as the judge, with a smile that mirrored their own, declared the Riggs the parents of Shantel Thompson.

The applause carried the weight of shared joy as Gary and Sharon's families, sitting in the gallery, clapped and cheered. Tears of happiness streamed down their faces, mingling with the echoes of their heartfelt congratulations. In that moment, all the years of yearning, disappointment, and resilience converged into a symphony of triumph.

Overwhelmed by a flood of emotions, Gary and Sharon rose from their seats, their eyes glistening with tears. They embraced tightly, their bodies pressed against each other, an unspoken acknowledgment of the love and dedication that had brought them to this point. In that embrace, they knew that their love for Shantel would be unwavering, an anchor for her in the stormy seas of life.

"Didn't I tell you, honey? There was no way they were going to say no to us."

"You were right," Sharon smiled. She knew she never should've doubted her husband. He was a prosecutor in the Mobile County court system and knew the ins and outs of the system. Still, Sharon couldn't shake the feeling that at any moment, something could go wrong. But that was all in the past. The judge declared Shantel was their daughter, pushing all Sharon's doubts behind her.

Amidst the swirling emotions, Sharon's gaze turned towards Shantel, who had already risen from her seat. In that instant, a mixture of anticipation and uncertainty etched across the young girl's face.

"Shantel, are you ready to go see your new home?" Sharon asked joyfully. Shantel, clutching her backpack, began walking towards the exit, leaving behind the couple who were now her parents.

"Shantel, wait," Sharon's voice, tinged with concern, pierced through the air, but Shantel remained resolute, deaf to the call. Doubt crept into Sharon's mind, and she turned to her husband, seeking reassurance. "What do you think that's all about?" She asked her husband.

"Sharon, we have to remember she's been through a lot at her young age. Everything is new to her. Give her some time. I'm sure she'll come around soon," Gary tried to reassure his wife.

Sharon nodded, her eyes moist with understanding. She knew that building a foundation of love and security would take time, that healing scars would be a gradual process. With renewed determination, she looked into Gary's eyes and exhaled deeply. Their hearts aligned in a shared resolve.

"It's time," Sharon said softly, her voice carrying a mix of vulnerability and determination. "Time to show Shantel what it means to have a loving family."

Arm in arm, Gary and Sharon left the courtroom, their hearts brimming with hope and the unwavering belief that their love would eventually reach the depths of the young girl's wounded soul. Their journey had just begun, and they were ready to provide Shantel with a home where love would blossom, healing would thrive, and dreams would flourish.

****

Shantel lay on her bed, engulfed in a shroud of impenetrable darkness that seemed to suffocate her. The weight of uncertainty pressed upon her, for this was her inaugural night in the Riggs' home, and its unfamiliarity loomed over her like a daunting specter. As her mother attempted to engage her in conversation during the drive home, Shantel withdrew into the recesses of her thoughts, cocooned in a self-imposed silence.

Upon arrival, Sharon and Gary led Shantel to her room, a sanctuary she hoped would provide respite from the world's prying eyes. Alas, Sharon's persistent knocks on the door shattered her reverie, each rap a reminder that solitude remained elusive. In her heart, Shantel yearned for an unspoken connection, silently pleading for Sharon to comprehend her unspoken desire to be left alone.

Though Shantel harbored no intention of rebuffing her parents, the harshness of her detachment stemmed from a deep-rooted pain. The memory of her birth parents' abandonment at the tender age of six cast an indelible shadow upon her soul. The fragments of their existence, once etched in her mind, now lay forgotten, obscured by the passage of time. The fleeting recollections of fleeting happiness, if they ever existed, eluded her grasp. The irrevocable act of leaving her alone in that desolate apartment, devoid of any means to find them, shattered her trust in their love. And now, as she gazed upon Sharon and Gary, she found herself grappling with the notion that their affection, too, may be ephemeral.

Amidst the tumult of emotions, one thought consumed Shantel's mind: the daunting prospect of ever bestowing her trust upon another.

Scarred by the wounds of her past, she questioned whether her heart could ever unfurl its fragile petals once more. Sharon and Gary, in all their kindness, might genuinely hold her dear as their own, but Shantel grappled with the unfathomable task of opening herself up to their love.

****

Sharon devoted herself wholeheartedly to bridging the chasm that separated Shantel from their newfound family. Week after week slipped away, and yet Shantel remained elusive, her guarded heart resisting the embrace of their love. The balmy embrace of summer enveloped them, and Sharon yearned to seize every moment, hoping that the warmth of the season would thaw the frost encasing Shantel's emotions. She longed for her daughter to blossom into a vibrant social butterfly, to form friendships that would weave a tapestry of joy into her life. But her endeavors yielded no discernible results, and Shantel seemed content to retreat into the solace of her room.

Undeterred by the mounting challenges, Sharon resolved to persevere. The arduous journey to parenthood had tested her patience, and she refused to relinquish the hope that Shantel would one day comprehend the boundless love that resided within their hearts. She would stop at nothing to forge an unbreakable bond, to unravel the enigma that shrouded Shantel's soul and reveal the luminous potential that lay dormant within.

"Shantel, I'm home!" Sharon's voice

reverberated through the halls, infused with a blend of anticipation and longing. She stood in the living room, her eyes fixed on the staircase, awaiting a response from the enigmatic girl who held her captive with every enigmatic glance.

With measured steps, Shantel descended the stairs, her gaze fixed upon Sharon, her silence an impenetrable fortress. The air crackled with unspoken words, a symphony of emotions hanging heavy in the room.

"Sorry for being away for so long. I had errands to run, and I picked this up for you on the way," Sharon explained, pulling out a box from her bag and extending it toward Shantel. A flicker of anticipation danced in her eyes, a plea for connection hidden beneath the surface.

Shantel's eyes darted from the doll nestled within the box to Sharon's expectant gaze. Confusion etched across her face as she grappled with the unexpected gesture. It wasn't her birthday, nor had she expressed any desire for a toy.

Realizing the absence of words from Shantel's lips, Sharon's hopes wavered, but she pressed on, determined to break through the barriers that held them captive. "I noticed you didn't have any toys when you came to live with us. I thought starting a doll collection might bring you some joy. What do you think?"

"Thanks," Shantel's voice, a mere whisper, hung in the air before she retreated back to the sanctuary of her room, closing the door behind her. A heavy sigh escaped Sharon's lips, a lament for the lack of progress that gnawed at her heart. Almost two months had passed since Shantel became a part of their lives, yet the path to understanding remained obstinately elusive.

****

As the remnants of their dinner settled, Sharon chose the opportune moment to broach her concerns with her husband. The quietude of the dining room enveloped them, providing a sanctuary for their earnest conversation. With a sense of purpose, she entered the room, bearing two steaming mugs of coffee, their delicate aroma mingling with the weight of her worries.

"Gary, can we delve into the matter of Shantel?" Sharon's voice carried a tinge of trepidation as she carefully placed the mugs on the table, their contents swirling with warmth.

Sensing the urgency in her tone, Gary's brows furrowed, mirroring his wife's concern. "What's troubling you? Did something transpire today?" His words hung in the air, laden with a genuine desire to understand the depths of Sharon's distress.

"That's precisely it. I can't shake the feeling that something is amiss with her. Today, I bought

Shantel a doll—a simple gesture of affection. Yet, her response was so detached. She merely thanked me and retreated to her room. It's as if she's built an impenetrable fortress around her emotions. Do you think we should seek professional help for her?"

Gary settled into his seat, his eyes meeting Sharon's as he sought to assuage her mounting anxiety. "Sweetie, I believe you might be reading too much into this. Shantel endured the heartache of abandonment at a tender age, and the circumstances of her early life remain shrouded in mystery. We can't fathom the extent of the trauma she's endured. Perhaps her guarded nature is a defense mechanism—a consequence of her painful past."

Sharon sank into her chair, her sigh carrying the weight of unspoken desires. "I yearn for her to embrace us, to open her heart to our love. All we want is to provide her with the warmth and care any loving parent would. Maybe I should shower her with more gifts, buy her presents to coax her out of her shell."

Gary interjected, his voice laced with gentle admonition. He couldn't help but feel a pang of frustration at Sharon's inclination to rely on material gestures to solve their familial challenges. While he was a successful prosecutor, hailing from a wealthy lineage, he recognized that true happiness lay beyond the realm of material possessions. Sharon's tendency to seek solace in lavish expenditures had become a familiar pattern —one he hoped to break.

"Sharon, remember that it's not about material possessions. Look at what Shantel carried with her when we adopted her—a suitcase full of clothes but devoid of toys. Perhaps she yearns for something deeper than mere playthings."

Perplexed, Sharon gazed at her husband, her mind spinning with possibilities. "Then, what does she truly desire? I'm running out of ideas to bridge the divide between us. Should I allow her to remain secluded in her room indefinitely? Come September, when she starts school, what if she withdraws further, refusing to engage with her peers?"

Gary absorbed his wife's words, his silence a testament to his careful consideration of her concerns. He understood the gravity of the situation. If Shantel remained reticent with them, the challenges might only amplify once she entered the school environment. Visions of daily visits to the principal's office, summoned to address Shantel's perceived difficulties, loomed before his eyes. There had to be a way to demonstrate unequivocally that Shantel was an integral part of their family—a way to ignite a spark of connection.

"I may have an idea," Gary finally spoke, his voice infused with a flicker of hope. "Perhaps what Shantel needs is a tangible demonstration that she truly belongs with us. Something that involves her directly in our lives."

Curiosity piqued, Sharon leaned forward, her eyes fixed on her husband. "Like what? What are you suggesting?"

Gary's thoughts crystallized, his plan taking shape. "Well, she still has a month before school begins. What if you involve her in your work? You've nurtured your passion for cultivating fruits, vegetables, and making jam, and it's evolved into a small business venture. What if you invite Shantel to assist you? Let her be a part of the process."

Sharon's mind whirred as she contemplated Gary's proposition. What had once been a hobby, a means of savoring the fruits of her labor, had blossomed into a burgeoning enterprise. Although their financial needs were more than met by Gary's profession, Sharon relished the satisfaction of generating supplementary income and indulging in occasional luxuries. She pondered whether Gary's suggestion held the key to unlocking

Shantel's reticence—if allowing her to participate in the labor of love that defined her own pursuits would elicit the dialogue they so desperately craved.

∞ ∞ ∞

Chapter 2

Sharon and Gary's unwavering devotion to Shantel was an undeniable force that radiated throughout the entire county. Their love for the abandoned girl was a spectacle that unfolded over the passing months, captivating the hearts of all who bore witness. Gary, a renowned prosecutor in town, became the harbinger of their extraordinary tale, as word of their benevolence and the profound act of opening their hearts and home to Shantel spread like wildfire.

The couple's compassion knew no bounds as they patiently guided Shantel towards finding her place within their family. Gone were the days when Sharon attempted to win Shantel's affection with material possessions; instead, she extended a heartfelt invitation for Shantel to assist her in her business endeavors. Initially, Shantel withdrew into the solitary confines of her room, hesitant to embrace this new opportunity. But one fateful day, much to Sharon's astonishment, Shantel emerged from her seclusion and softly inquired if she could lend a hand in canning the goods.

Sharon was profoundly moved by Shantel's

unexpected request, her heart now more receptive to accepting the assistance. Yet, their conversations were limited, halted at the threshold of banal exchanges. Each morning, Shantel ventured into the kitchen, her presence a silent vow to aid Sharon. Countless times, Sharon yearned to break the silence, to bridge the gap between them with words of warmth.

However, she heeded her husband's counsel, remembering his wise words, "Let Shantel be the one to speak first. That way, you'll know what she wants to talk about." And thus, Sharon abided by this advice, toiling alongside Shantel in companionable silence. Their progress may have been gradual, but it was progress nonetheless.

Yet, Sharon's apprehension loomed like a shadow, casting doubt upon what lay ahead when Shantel would commence her schooling. She feared that Shantel's self-imposed silence would hinder her interactions not only with fellow students but also with her teachers. Gary, however, assuaged her concerns, assuring her that they would engage in open dialogue with the principal and educators, apprising them of the obstacles they faced with Shantel. With bated breath, Sharon yearned for September to arrive, hoping that the commencement of school would dissolve Shantel's fear of communication, allowing her to recognize the abundant love that enveloped her within this family, a love that would never abandon her.

Behind his stoic facade, Gary grappled

with his own insecurities, his worry for Shantel mirroring Sharon's fears. Each day at the office, he tirelessly pondered strategies to coax Shantel out of her shell, yearning for her to embrace them fully. Yet, the perfect actions and words eluded him, slipping through his fingers like ephemeral fragments of a dream. Though he observed flickers of progress—Shantel uttering more words and assisting Sharon with her business—she remained ensconced in the sanctuary of her room for the majority of her time. Gary clung to the hope that once she embarked on her educational journey, the walls she built around herself would crumble, and she would emerge as a social butterfly. In the interim, he and Sharon pledged unwavering love and support, patiently awaiting the moment when Shantel would unveil her readiness to embrace a deeper connection with their family.

****

As September unfurled its vibrant tapestry, an undercurrent of trepidation coursed through Gary and Sharon's veins, for Shantel exhibited no trace of anticipation for the impending school year. Their desperate attempts to dismantle the fortress she had erected around herself proved futile, as she remained an enigma, her inner world veiled from their reach. In a last-ditch effort to breach this emotional barrier, Sharon clung to the hope that a mother-daughter shopping excursion would serve as a catalyst for change.

"Shantel, it's time to find clothes for school," Sharon gently beckoned, leading her daughter into the bustling store. "Now, I'm not sure what style resonates with you, which is why I want you to choose whatever your heart desires," she beamed, her eyes brimming with affection.

"What about the clothes I already have?" Shantel's hesitant inquiry hung in the air, a fragile thread connecting her past to the present.

Sharon's heart soared with a symphony of emotions. Those six words strung together in a sentence were a resplendent melody, the most profound utterance Shantel had bestowed upon her since the day they welcomed her into their lives. Simultaneously, Sharon's heart shattered, realizing that Shantel believed her existing garments sufficed, oblivious to the necessity of acquiring new attire for the commencement of school. A surge of maternal yearning propelled Sharon to guide her daughter gently, steering her away from the shadows of her past.

"Sweetie, it's important to have fresh outfits for school. You deserve to embark on this new chapter in attire that reflects your vibrant spirit. Don't you want to make a striking first impression on your new teachers?" Sharon's voice resonated with warmth and genuine concern, weaving a tapestry of hope.

"I suppose," Shantel mumbled, her shoulders shrugging nonchalantly. "I don't remember attending school before my parents," she admitted, her gaze averted, the weight of an unfinished thought lingering in the air.

"Shantel, that chapter of your life has faded into the recesses of the past. There is no sense in dwelling on what cannot be changed. Let us seize this opportunity to create new memories, to relish in the joy of shopping together," Sharon whispered, her voice a soothing balm, an invitation to embrace the present moment.

****

As the sun dipped below the horizon, casting a warm glow over the tranquil abode, Gary inquired about the outcome of their mother-daughter shopping expedition.

"Did the two of you have fun shopping?"

Sharon, her heart brimming with a mixture of elation and cautious optimism, requested a moment alone with her husband, urging Shantel to retreat to her room and unpack her newfound treasures.

"Shantel, why don't you go put your clothes away while I talk to your father," Sharon said.

"Okay," Shantel rushed to her room.

With an intrigued quirk of his eyebrow,

Gary regarded his wife intently. As he departed for work earlier that day, a foreboding premonition had nestled within his consciousness, apprehensive of the challenges Sharon might encounter while navigating the labyrinthine corridors of Shantel's reticence. Yet, what unfolded before his eyes surpassed his wildest expectations, an unforeseen marvel that defied the bounds of his imagination.

"Please, enlighten me," he implored, his voice a delicate tapestry of curiosity and anticipation.

"Gary, I hesitate to proclaim that I've shattered the impenetrable barrier she enveloped herself in, for it remains a work in progress, a delicate dance of trust. But what transpired today, it was a glimmer of hope, a nascent ray of light," Sharon began, her voice a tender whisper, laden with profound emotion. "When I informed her that new clothes were essential for the upcoming school year, she was taken aback, her eyes betraying a flicker of disbelief. She confided that she possesses no recollection of ever attending school before, a testament to the profound scars etched upon her soul by her tumultuous past. No wonder she has been hesitant to unfurl the tendrils of her heart within our embrace."

Gary's gaze softened, his arms enveloping Sharon in a gesture of solace and reassurance. "From what I witnessed today, my love, I dare say she is slowly casting aside the shackles of her fear, inching toward the precipice of vulnerability. She is beginning to comprehend that we shall never abandon her, which our love shall stand as an unwavering fortress in her tumultuous world."

A tremor of hope reverberated through Sharon's voice as she continued, her words a poignant plea for the future. "My fervent prayer is that we continue to progress, to traverse this intricate path hand in hand. May she continue to unveil fragments of herself, a mosaic of trust and resilience. Let us forge ahead, nurturing the delicate tendrils of connection, ensuring that our journey remains one of forward momentum, rather than regression."

Tears glistened in Gary's eyes as he gazed upon his wife, a profound conviction etched upon his features. "Sharon, I hold an unwavering belief that this tapestry of love and healing shall only grow richer with time. We are on the precipice of realizing the dreams we cherished for so long, witnessing the birth of the family we yearned to create."

And in that tender moment, within the sanctity of their embrace, they vowed to traverse this path together, their hearts entwined with the indomitable spirit of Shantel, as they embarked on a journey of healing, love, and the boundless potential of a newfound family.

****

Sharon marveled at the progress they had made with Shantel, her heart swelling with a blend of pride and concern. While school remained a challenge, with the principal summoning them for meetings to discuss Shantel's social interactions - or lack thereof - Gary staunchly defended their daughter, underscoring the lingering effects of her difficult early life. Sharon found solace in the fact that preparing Shantel for school each morning was a seamless task, but she understood that forging friendships would demand time and patience.

A vibrant Saturday morning unfolded, with the sun casting its golden rays through the kitchen window, painting the room with a warm, autumnal glow. Sharon longed for Shantel to embrace the company of peers her age, but the young girl still gravitated towards solitude, the echoes of her past reverberating in her present. However, one notable change had emerged since Shantel's arrival—the desire to emerge from her room and engage in sporadic conversations with her parents. Though fleeting, these moments of connection represented a glimmer of progress, a testament to the resilient spirit nestled within her daughter's heart.

"Mum?" Shantel's voice wafted downstairs, a delicate melody that caressed Sharon's ears, reminding her of the profound transformation they had undergone as a family.

"Yes, my sweet girl," Sharon responded, her heart swelling with a profound sense of fulfillment. No matter how many times she heard Shantel address her as "mom," the words carried an indescribable weight, an affirmation of the family they had longed for, a testament to their enduring love.

Shantel's voice beckoned her mother from the depths of her reverie, pulling Sharon back to the present moment, her laughter dancing in the air like a playful sprite. With a gentle chuckle, Sharon brushed away the wisps of distraction, her eyes focused on her daughter. "I apologize, my thoughts wandered. What did you need, my dear?"

"Can I go outside and play?" Shantel queried, her eyes shining with anticipation. "I want to swing on the beautiful swing set you and Dad built for me."

Sharon and Gary had spared no expense in creating a haven of childhood wonderment for their beloved daughter. When they noticed Shantel's hesitance to engage with her classmates, Gary took it upon himself to construct a swing set that surpassed all expectations. It stood as a testament to their commitment to providing Shantel with an immersive childhood experience.

This swing set was no ordinary structure found in front yards—no, it was a kaleidoscope of joy, complete with a slide, monkey bars, and an array of playful embellishments reminiscent of a whimsical playground.

Sharon gazed out the window, the sun's rays casting a halo around her daughter's figure. With a nod of approval, she replied, "The weather is delightful, my dear. Go forth and revel in its embrace. But remember to stay in the front yard, where I can keep a watchful eye on you."

Shantel donned her coat, her smile radiant as a thousand sunbeams. "I am truly fortunate to have two parents who love and care for me. I had always hoped to find people like you and Dad," she whispered, her words carrying the weight of a thousand unspoken dreams.

Sharon stood rooted to her spot in the kitchen, her eyes fixed on Shantel as she soared through the air on the swings, laughter cascading like a symphony of joy. The transformation that had unfolded before their eyes was nothing short of miraculous. A mere few months ago, Shantel had been a hesitant, withdrawn soul, and now she radiated with an effervescence that seemed almost surreal. Sharon allowed herself a tender laugh, reminiscing about the day they first brought Shantel home, finding it difficult to fathom that this vibrant, spirited girl was the same child they had welcomed into their lives.

The melodic chime of the kitchen timer interrupted Sharon's reverie, signaling the completion of her laundry. Instinctively, she glanced towards the back of the house, where the laundry room resided. The momentary dilemma tugged at her heart—should she leave Shantel's side even for a brief moment? Yet, rationality interceded, reminding her that their neighborhood in Mobile, Alabama, was a haven of tranquility, free from the grip of worry.

"I shall not disturb her mirth," Sharon resolved, a glimmer of maternal trust guiding her decision. "She is reveling in her joy, and what harm could befall her in our idyllic haven? I shall retrieve my laundry from the dryer and be back in an instant."

With a final gaze cast upon her daughter, Sharon departed for the laundry room, her heart buoyed by the belief that their lives had blossomed into a tapestry of love, hope, and the boundless potential of a family united.

****

Shantel reveled in the sheer exhilaration of soaring through the air on the swings, her heart alight with unadulterated joy. This was her sanctuary, the place where she sought solace from the relentless torment of her classmates at school. The reasons for her seclusion remained unspoken, concealed within the tender recesses of her wounded heart. They didn't want to be her friends - this painful truth echoed in her mind, etched into her very being.

From the moment she stepped foot into the school, whispers of her past followed her like a shadow. The rumor mill churned with tales of her abandonment, circulating through the small town until they reached the ears of Sharon and Gary, who, with boundless love and compassion, welcomed her into their family. Yet, the unkindness of ten-year-olds proved relentless, their taunts a constant reminder of her perceived otherness. Shantel, wise beyond her years, understood the cruel dynamics of childhood cliques, and it was no wonder she sought refuge in the solitude of the swings, far removed from the piercing barbs of her classmates.

With each pendulum-like motion, Shantel's voice soared through the crisp air, her screams mingling with the winds of freedom. The exhilaration of her flight held an unspoken defiance, a silent proclamation that she refused to succumb to the ridicule that haunted her existence. She knew full well that if any of her classmates were to witness her now, they would mock her, branding her a mere child. The swings, it seemed, were reserved exclusively for her—a sacred haven where she could reclaim her sense of self away from the prying eyes of her tormentors.

But then, a sudden interruption shattered the tranquility of her respite. Shantel's eyes, filled with curiosity and a hint of apprehension, caught sight of a stranger venturing onto their front lawn. A surge of unease rippled through her, for she had never laid eyes on this man before. Yet, she reasoned that it could be an innocent encounter —a visitor seeking her father's legal expertise, a common occurrence given Gary's occupation as a prosecutor.

Halting her swinging momentum, Shantel approached the stranger with a blend of caution and inquisitiveness. "Excuse me, sir. Can I assist you in any way?"

A warm smile graced the man's face, his eyes reflecting a gentle sincerity. "Hello," he greeted, his voice laced with an air of relief. "I'm grateful to have found someone to talk to. You see, I seem to have lost my way. Can you provide me with directions to Dauphin Island?"

The unexpected query lingered in the air, casting a momentary shadow over Shantel's youthful countenance. Her mind whirred with a blend of concern and curiosity, questioning the intentions of this unfamiliar face. Yet, her compassionate nature urged her to extend a helping hand, to offer guidance to a stranger in need.

∞ ∞ ∞

Chapter 3

The evening sky gradually darkened, casting a somber ambiance over Sharon's surroundings. Time slipped away from her as she became engrossed in various household tasks after fetching the laundry. As a result, she made the decision to allow her daughter, Shantel, to linger outside a little longer. Trusting her daughter's responsible nature, Sharon believed that Shantel would seek shelter indoors as the night grew late.

Moments later, the sound of the front door opening reached Sharon's ears, causing her to pause mid-action. Assuming it was Shantel returning inside, she turned towards the kitchen, ready to inform her daughter that dinner would soon be served. However, her anticipation turned to surprise when she laid eyes on Gary instead.

"Oh, I thought you were Shantel," Sharon's voice trailed off, momentarily taken aback by the unexpected sight. "Would you mind finding her and asking her to come in? Dinner is nearly ready." She approached her husband, planting a gentle kiss upon his cheek.

Gary's expression revealed confusion. "Why would I need to fetch her?" he inquired, his brow furrowing in perplexity.

"She's still outside, playing on the swings," Sharon replied, her tone laced with a tinge of certainty.

Gary shook his head, a sense of concern beginning to take hold. "She wasn't outside when I arrived home," he disclosed, his words conveying an unsettling truth.

"I suppose she must have come inside while I was in the basement," Sharon conjectured, her thoughts racing. Without hesitation, she made her way towards the stairs, her voice echoing through the house. "Shantel! It's time for dinner!"

As the silence persisted, Sharon's worry burgeoned, permeating the air. Sensing the urgency, she dashed upstairs to Shantel's room, her heart pounding in her chest. Throwing open the door, she let out a piercing cry, the magnitude of her anguish evident. . "GARY! GARY! CALL THE COPS!" she screamed, her voice quivering with fear.

Startled by his wife's distress, Gary hurried to Shantel's room, freezing in the doorway as he beheld the desolate space before him. The emptiness engulfed him, a chilling realization settling deep within his soul.

"She's... she's missing," Sharon's voice trembled, her words laced with despair.

Summoning his resolve, Gary fought to conceal his own mounting apprehension. "Stay calm. I'm sure she's somewhere nearby," he reassured, his voice steady. Descending the stairs, he hastened to grab the phone, dialing the emergency number with a trembling hand.

"911. What's your emergency?" came the voice of the operator on the other end.

"My daughter... she's gone," Gary uttered, gesturing for Sharon to take the phone. She was the last one to have seen Shantel, and it was crucial for her to provide the necessary details. "My wife can provide more information."

Taking a deep breath, Sharon accepted the phone, her voice quavering as she attempted to compose herself. "Yes?" she managed to say, her voice filled with a mix of desperation and hope.

"Your husband informed us that your daughter is missing. Can you please provide additional details?" the operator inquired, her tone compassionate yet professional.

"She went outside to play in our front yard, around four in the afternoon," Sharon began, her voice trembling with emotion. "I was keeping an eye on her until I had to attend to something in the back of the house. I assumed she had returned indoors as darkness descended, but she wasn't in her room. And my husband didn't spot her outside when he returned from work," Sharon's words were punctuated by tears. "Please, we implore you, help us find our daughter."

"Ma'am, I understand this is an incredibly distressing situation for you, but please try to remain calm," the operator soothingly responded. "We have already dispatched a patrol car, and it should arrive at your location within a few minutes. Until then, I urge you not to panic."

With a heavy heart, Sharon ended the call and approached Gary, seeking solace in his arms. He enveloped her in a comforting embrace, pressing a tender kiss upon the crown of her head. "We will find her," he whispered, his voice filled with determination. "The police will do everything in their power to bring her back to us."

*****

Sharon found herself trapped in the depths of despair during the arduous days of the search for Shantel. Every passing moment seemed to stretch into an eternity of anguish. Gary, realizing the extent of his wife's distress, took time off from work, joining the collective effort of the entire community, determined to aid the authorities in finding their beloved daughter. Despite the relentless efforts, two long weeks had passed without any semblance of an update. The weight of uncertainty bore down heavily upon Sharon, testing her patience with each passing day.

Restless and consumed by a sense of helplessness, Sharon's frustration reached a boiling point. In a fit of despair, she slammed her hands down on the kitchen table, the sound reverberating through the room. "I can't bear sitting here, doing nothing!" she exclaimed, her voice trembling with a mix of desperation and anger. "The police are taking an eternity to find her."

Gary, ever the voice of reason, attempted to assuage Sharon's mounting distress. "They assured us they would contact us as soon as they have an update," he reminded her, his voice filled with a mixture of empathy and concern.

"Two weeks!" Sharon's voice cracked with the weight of her emotions. "It has been two agonizing weeks, Gary! The longer she remains missing, the direr the outcome becomes." Tears streamed down her face as she uttered her deepest fears. "If she was going to come back, she would have by now."

Gary was about to respond when the shrill ring of the phone pierced the air, causing both of them to tense with anticipation. Instinctively, he reached out, gently halting Sharon from answering. His intuition told him that the call was from the police, and the news they were about to receive wouldn't be favorable. Protecting Sharon from the unbearable weight of the moment, he took it upon himself to answer the call.

"Hello?" Gary's voice quivered, his heart pounding in his chest. The gravity of the situation hung heavy in the air.

"Mr. Riggs? This is Officer Ruark," came the voice on the other end of the line, a tinge of solemnity coloring each word.

"Yes, officer. Do you have news about our daughter?" Gary's voice trembled, a mix of apprehension and hope woven into his words.

"I do," Officer Ruark responded, his voice carrying a hint of reluctance. "But it would be better if I spoke to you and your wife in person, at the station."

Gary's heart sank, his worst fears solidifying with each passing second. He turned to face Sharon, his voice filled with a mixture of sorrow and resolve. "Officer Ruark wants us to come to the station to speak with him," he relayed, his gaze filled with compassion.

Sharon's tears flowed freely as she nodded, her heart gripped by an all-encompassing dread. Gary encircled her in a comforting embrace, their steps heavy and laden with sorrow as they made their way out of their home and into the waiting car. Officer Ruark stood patiently, a somber figure, waiting for them at the station.

"Mr. and Mrs. Riggs, please follow me," Officer Ruark beckoned, leading them through the corridors of the station. His office awaited them, a sanctuary of solace amidst the whirlwind of emotions that swirled within. On his desk, a box of tissues stood as a testament to the countless heart-wrenching conversations he had witnessed. "Thank you for coming in. Now, as I mentioned on the phone, we have an update on Shantel." He paused, a heavy silence filling the room, brimming with unspoken words. "I had hoped this wouldn't be the kind of news I had to deliver, but her body was discovered on the beach."

The word "body" hung in the air like a shroud of sorrow, evoking a torrent of anguish from Sharon. Her voice cracked as she struggled to utter the painful truth. "That means... she's..." The word caught in her throat, the mere act of speaking it making the reality all too real. If she dared to say it aloud, it would mean accepting that Shantel was truly gone.

"I am deeply sorry." Officer Ruark's expression shifted, his eyes filled with empathy. "We believe she was killed elsewhere, her life stolen from her. The perpetrator callously discarded her body on the beach, perhaps hoping it would be consumed by the vastness of the ocean. However, fate dictated otherwise, and she was found lying in the sand. Further tests will provide more answers, but we suspect she had already succumbed to her fate for several hours before being abandoned on the shore," Officer Ruark somberly explained, his words etched with a profound sorrow.

Sharon's heart trembled beneath the weight of her sorrow, tears streaming down her face unchecked. The anguish that enveloped her was unfathomable as she grappled with the unimaginable horrors her daughter had endured.

The thought of Shantel, her precious child, being callously discarded on the beach like a mere piece of garbage sent waves of anguish crashing through her soul.

Gary, his voice filled with a mixture of anguish and determination, broke the heavy silence. "Who could commit such an unspeakable act against our daughter?" His words hung in the air, infused with a potent blend of grief and righteous anger.

Officer Ruark, his expression etched with empathy, responded with a somber tone. "We have a suspect in this case, Anthony Welch. There have been reports of him attempting to kidnap children within the town. We've been tirelessly searching for him, but he always manages to elude us. Thankfully, we do have descriptions from witnesses, and our officers are actively scouring the area in pursuit of him."

Gary, his intuition keenly attuned to the nuances of law enforcement, sensed that Officer Ruark was withholding information. "There's more to this, isn't there?" he inquired, his voice laden with a mixture of suspicion and concern. He knew all too well the tendency of authorities to shield families from certain details.

Sharon's anguish cut through the air as she cried out, her voice trembling with a potent mix of grief and frustration. "What does it matter now? Our daughter is gone, and she will never return! I don't care about the details. I just want to see this man pay for what he did to Shantel!"

Officer Ruark, his voice laced with compassion, sought to reassure the devastated parents. "Mrs. Riggs, I want to assure you that we are doing everything within our power to apprehend the person responsible for your daughter's murder. We must tread carefully to ensure that we capture the right individual. Anthony Welch is currently our primary suspect, but we must gather all the evidence to ensure a solid case."

Sharon's anger flared, her voice cutting through the air like a sharp blade. "What do you mean, 'the right man'? You just said he's a suspect. What more proof do you need?"

Officer Ruark, his gaze steady, explained the complexities of the investigation. "It's not as simple as it may seem. Shantel was found on the beach, already deceased. That means we need to determine where she was killed to gather crucial evidence. At this moment, one of our officers is at your house, searching for any clues on the front lawn where she was last seen."

Sharon's disbelief mingled with her tears

as she spoke with mounting frustration. "I can't believe this. Our daughter was taken from us, and it feels like nothing is being done!"

Gary, his voice filled with a mixture of wisdom and empathy, sought to calm his anguished wife. "Sweetie, I've seen similar situations unfold in court. The authorities need to gather all the evidence before making an arrest, especially in cases as grave as this involving kidnapping and murder."

Sharon's anger surged forth, her voice quivering with indignation. "How can you take their side? They tell me there's a suspect, and yet they can't arrest him because they're not sure!"

Officer Ruark, his demeanor resolute, attempted to explain the intricate process of the investigation. "Mrs. Riggs, as your husband mentioned, we must ensure that we have a solid foundation of evidence before making an arrest. Anthony Welch is indeed the main suspect, but we must be thorough. One significant challenge we face is the lack of a weapon. Nothing was found with Shantel's body, and if we don't find any evidence in your yard, it will make the investigation more challenging. Furthermore, we are awaiting test results to determine the cause of her death. Once we receive that information, it will provide crucial insights into the case."

As if on cue, Officer Ruark's phone rang, shattering the heavy silence that enveloped the room. He picked it up, his eyes focused and attentive. "Officer Ruark speaking."

"Ruark, it's Griffith. I'm leaving the Riggs' property now. We didn't find a weapon, but we discovered blood on the grass. We've collected the specific blades of grass where the blood was found and sent them to the lab for analysis."

"Thank you, Officer Griffith. Please inform me immediately if you find any additional evidence," Officer Ruark responded, his voice filled with a mix of gratitude and anticipation. He hung up the phone and turned his gaze back to the grieving couple. "That was Officer Griffith, who conducted the search at your residence. We discovered blood on the grass, which will help us establish a timeline for when the crime occurred."

Sharon, her voice trembling with a blend of hope and desperation, interjected, unable to suppress her frustration any longer. "But what about the blood? Isn't that the proof you need to arrest him?" Her tone was filled with a mixture of disbelief and impatience, unable to comprehend why the officer seemed to downplay this crucial discovery.

Officer Ruark, his countenance grave yet resolute, met Sharon's gaze with empathy. "Mrs. Riggs, the presence of blood is indeed a significant development. It indicates that Shantel was either killed or attacked in your yard, which provides us with a critical piece of the puzzle. However, what we need to do next is send the blood samples for testing. This analysis will help us determine whether the blood belongs to Shantel or the perpetrator. If we can ascertain that the blood belongs to the killer, it will serve as a vital piece of evidence, narrowing down our search and aiding in the identification and arrest of the responsible party."

The weight of the investigation's intricacies hung heavy in the room, as the grieving parents grappled with a myriad of emotions. Each passing moment brought them closer to the truth, yet the journey ahead seemed insurmountable. In their eyes, justice wore a fragile cloak, and the resolution they desperately sought remained tantalizingly out of reach.

Sharon's trembling heart was gripped by disbelief as Officer Ruark's words sank in. The weight of the situation slowly settled upon her shoulders, and she began to comprehend the complexities that hindered an immediate arrest. The anger that had initially been directed at the police now turned inward, transforming into a searing self-blame that consumed her. "How could I have been so careless?" she lamented, her voice filled with a profound sense of guilt. "I should have never allowed her to play outside when I couldn't keep a constant watch from the window."

Officer Ruark, his tone laced with empathy, sought to console Sharon in her moment of anguish. "Please, Mrs. Riggs, do not burden yourself with guilt. Tragedies like this are never something a parent can foresee. There are individuals in this world who harbor unthinkable darkness, and their actions cannot be attributed to your actions as a mother."

Sharon shook her head, engulfed in a swirling vortex of guilt and remorse. Each thought, each memory, fueled her conviction that she had failed her daughter. "Why didn't I hear her scream?" she questioned, her voice trembling with self-doubt. "If she was attacked outside our home, I should have heard her cries for help. Unless..."

Her words hung in the air, pregnant with a dreadful realization. Gary, sensing his wife's torment, gently prompted her to share her thoughts. "What is it, Sharon? What has crossed your mind?"

Tears welled in Sharon's eyes as she uttered her darkest fear. "She could have been screaming for help while I was in the basement. The sound wouldn't have reached my ears, and I failed to protect her."

Officer Ruark, his voice calm and measured,

interjected. "Mr. Riggs, I believe it would be best for your wife to return home for now. We will keep you both informed about any developments in the investigation. And please, recognize that none of this rests on your shoulders. You are not to blame."

Sharon longed to believe the officer's reassurances, but the weight of her guilt bore down upon her like an oppressive burden. The knowledge that her daughter's killer remained at large fueled her determination to seek justice. Whoever had committed this heinous act deserved to be apprehended and held accountable for the rest of their days.

Throughout the following days, Sharon's mind became consumed by a maelstrom of emotions. She grappled with the guilt that gnawed at her conscience, vowing to herself that she would not find solace until the perpetrator faced the consequences of their actions. Each night, darkness enveloped her as she lay in bed, her mind haunted by the memory of Shantel's innocent face. The vividness of their last moments together contrasted sharply with the cold reality of her daughter's absence.

The relentless passage of time continued to gnaw at Sharon's spirit, each day stretching out before her like an eternity. She devoured news reports, searching for any sign of progress in the investigation. The faces of her daughter and the suspected killer stared back at her from the television screen, a stark juxtaposition of innocence and malevolence.

In the depths of her soul, Sharon held tightly to her conviction that the perpetrator would be apprehended. Each day, she found solace in the pursuit of justice, even as the pain of her loss threatened to consume her. She clung to the memories of Shantel, willing herself to carry on in the face of insurmountable sorrow.

****

Officer Ruark leaned against the bathroom wall, his heart heavy with grief. The memories of the Riggs family's tragedy flooded his mind, intertwining with the image of his own daughter's innocent embrace. The stark contrast between the warmth of his homecoming and the desolation that awaited the Riggs family struck him with a profound sense of injustice.

Tears welled up in Officer Ruark's eyes, blurring his vision as he tried to make sense of the senseless. The weight of his duty pressed upon him, the burden of protecting his community and bringing justice to those who had suffered. But in that moment, alone with his thoughts, he allowed himself to surrender to the raw emotions that had been building within him.

The sound of his wife's gentle knocks on the door interrupted his solitude, snapping him back to the present. He hastily wiped away his tears, trying to compose himself before facing her. Taking a deep breath, he unlocked the door and stepped out, wearing a forced smile that barely concealed his inner turmoil.

His wife looked at him with concern, her eyes searching for answers. "John, what happened? You rushed in here so suddenly," she asked, her voice tinged with worry.

Officer Ruark glanced at her, his gaze filled with a mixture of sadness and determination. "It's nothing, honey," he replied, his voice strained. "Just... just a tough day at work."

She furrowed her brow, unconvinced. "John, I know when something is bothering you. Please, talk to me. I'm here for you."

He reached out and gently grasped her hand, appreciating her unwavering support. "I... I witnessed something today, something that reminded me of how fragile life can be," he admitted, his voice quivering with suppressed emotion. "It's difficult to comprehend the pain that the Riggs family is going through. Their daughter... she was taken from them, just like that."

His wife's eyes widened, her own heart heavy with empathy. "Oh, John, how devastating. I can't even begin to imagine."

Officer Ruark nodded, his voice filled with a mix of sorrow and determination. "Neither can I, but it's my duty to find the person responsible for this. No family should have to endure such a tragedy."

His wife squeezed his hand, her love and support palpable. "You're a good man, John. The strength you carry is extraordinary. Just remember, you're not alone in this. Lean on me when you need to."

A flicker of gratitude crossed Officer Ruark's eyes as he looked at his wife, his partner through thick and thin. In that moment, he felt a renewed sense of purpose, knowing that he had someone to share both the burden and the triumphs that lay ahead.

Together, they stood in silent solidarity, drawing strength from each other, ready to face the challenges of the days to come.

******

As Officer Ruark lay in bed beside his sleeping wife, the weight of his troubled thoughts kept him awake. The moonlight filtered through the curtains, casting haunting shadows on the walls, as his mind wandered back to the cases he had unraveled throughout his career. Each recollection carried its own weight, vivid and dramatic, etched into his memory.

He remembered the chilling case of a serial arsonist who had terrorized the city, leaving a trail of destruction in his wake. The flames licked the night sky, devouring homes and dreams with merciless intensity. Officer Ruark had tirelessly pursued the twisted mind behind the fires, determined to bring an end to the reign of terror. The memories of charred ruins and tear-stained faces of the victims haunted him still, but he found solace in knowing that justice had prevailed and the city could begin to heal.

Another memory surged forward, seeping into his consciousness. It was the heart-wrenching case of a missing child, a little boy who had disappeared without a trace. Officer Ruark recalled the frantic searches, the anguished pleas of the parents, and the relentless pursuit of every lead. Nights turned into days, and hope hung by a thread. But in the end, a break in the case led Officer Ruark to a hidden basement, where the innocent child had been held captive. The moment he saw the boy's tear-stained face, trembling but alive, Officer Ruark felt a mix of relief and fury, vowing to protect every child from the darkness that had tried to consume them.

A third memory emerged, casting a shadow over his thoughts. It was the haunting case of a brutal murder that had shaken the community to its core. Officer Ruark vividly recalled the grisly crime scene, the blood-soaked room, and the palpable fear that permeated the air. Hours turned into days, and the investigation led him down a twisted path of secrets and lies. But with unwavering determination, he pieced together the puzzle until the truth was exposed. The moment the cuffs were locked around the wrists of the killer, Officer Ruark felt a profound mix of satisfaction and sorrow, knowing that justice had been served, but a life had been irrevocably lost.

Each recollection intertwined with the weight of the present, reminding Officer Ruark of the immense responsibility he bore. The faces of the victims, the cries of their loved ones, and the relentless pursuit of justice lingered in his mind. He knew that the Riggs family's tragedy would join the tapestry of these memories, fueling his resolve to bring solace to their shattered lives.

Beside him, his wife stirred in her sleep, a small sigh escaping her lips. Officer Ruark gently reached out and brushed a strand of hair away from her face, finding comfort in her presence. He vowed to carry the weight of his past cases with him, allowing their echoes to guide him in the pursuit of truth and justice, as he navigated the treacherous roads of darkness, bringing light to those who needed it most.

∞ ∞ ∞

Chapter 4

Sharon's heart ached with an unyielding desire for justice, her desperation intensifying with each passing day. The sluggish pace of the police investigation gnawed at her, leaving her restless and unsatisfied. Gary, her husband, attempted to assuage her fears, urging patience as he believed that time would bring about the resolution they sought. But Sharon couldn't bear such placidity; she yearned for swift action, for the man responsible for her daughter's untimely demise to be apprehended and locked away. She couldn't fathom how Anthony Welch, the perpetrator of such a heinous act, could continue to exist unperturbed by the weight of his actions.

On a particularly sorrowful day, Sharon found herself seated in the somber embrace of her living room, tears cascading down her cheeks as they had done so many times before. The shrill ring of the phone pierced through her anguish, causing her heart to skip a beat. With a mix of trepidation and hope, she sprang to her feet, snatching the receiver in her trembling hand.

"Hello?" Her voice quivered, a manifestation of her fragile emotions. She dared not allow herself to hope, having been deceived by false promises in the past. The sting of disappointment lingered in her memory.

"Mrs. Riggs, this is Officer Ruark," a solemn voice on the other end of the line spoke. "We have Anthony Welch in custody."

The words hung in the air, momentarily suspended in disbelief. Sharon's mind struggled to process the magnitude of what she had just heard. "You... you caught him?" she managed to utter, her voice a fragile thread of hope.

"We did," Officer Ruark confirmed, his tone carrying a mix of professional detachment and empathetic understanding. "I'm calling to inform you that he is scheduled to go on trial next week. However, I must caution you that this case presents challenges. We still lack a motive, and a weapon was never recovered."

Sharon's fears, though anticipated, clawed their way to the surface. She knew the absence of a motive and physical evidence could complicate the proceedings. Yet, she clung to the belief that the court system would unveil the truth, that the jury would peer beyond the gaps and convict Anthony Welch for the merciless murder of an innocent child.

Gratitude welled up within her, mingling with a deep sense of relief. "Thank you, Officer. I cannot express how relieved I am that you finally caught him. I will inform my husband of this news. It means the world to us."

As the call ended, Sharon's heart brimmed with bittersweet emotions. The journey toward justice had commenced, and though uncertainty loomed, a flicker of hope burned within her, igniting a newfound determination to see her daughter's killer held accountable for the irreversible pain he had inflicted upon their lives.

****

Three agonizing weeks had crawled by, and now Sharon and her husband found themselves seated in the solemn courtroom, their hearts pounding with anticipation as they awaited the verdict that would determine the fate of Anthony Welch. The passing days had been a torturous ordeal for the couple, leaving them emotionally drained and apprehensive. Sharon's gut twisted with an ominous premonition as she watched the jury return to the room after half an hour of deliberation, their expressions inscrutable.

"We find the defendant not guilty," a juror declared, handing over the damning piece of paper to the judge.

A surge of disbelief and despair coursed through Sharon's veins, threatening to overwhelm her. Louis Stewart, Anthony's smug-faced lawyer, reveled in his apparent triumph, well aware that he had secured his client's freedom despite the accusation of murder.

Judge Barrette cast a sympathetic glance toward the devastated parents as she heard Sharon's anguished wail upon hearing the verdict. Her heart ached for the mother, but she was bound by the jury's decision, constrained by the lack of evidence that had ultimately swayed the case.

"Mr. and Mrs. Riggs, allow me to extend my deepest condolences for the loss of your daughter," Judge Barrette spoke with a somber tone, her voice laced with empathy. "I understand that today's outcome is far from what you had hoped for. However, the jury, considering the absence of evidence and motive, has reached their decision. Mr. Welch, you are free to go."

Gary, offering a small semblance of solace, wrapped his arm around Sharon's trembling form as they stepped outside the courthouse. The news of the verdict had spread like wildfire, and a throng of people had gathered, their expectant faces filled with hope for justice. But the expression on Gary's face and the tears shimmering in his eyes shattered their anticipation, igniting a collective outcry.

"MURDERER!" The crowd erupted into chants as Anthony emerged from the courthouse, a free man. "MURDERER! MURDERER!"

Sharon couldn't bear the presence of these people, knowing that her fragile composure could crumble at any moment. The hope that had accompanied her arrival at the courthouse that morning had been mercilessly crushed. Gary guided her into the car, his touch offering a measure of comfort. "Let's go home," he whispered, tenderly planting a kiss on the top of her head before starting the engine.

Silent tears streamed down Sharon's face as she stared out of the car window, her gaze locked on the man who had callously robbed her daughter of life. Anthony stood outside the courthouse, embracing his lawyer with a sense of triumph. He believed he had successfully evaded the consequences of his heinous act. But Sharon knew the truth, and the weight of that knowledge only intensified her grief. It was unjust—a bitter realization that pierced her heart. The man who had stolen her daughter's future was now free, devoid of remorse. Meanwhile, Shantel's life had been ruthlessly truncated, denied the chance to flourish.

The journey home was marked by a profound silence, as Sharon harbored no inclination to engage in conversation. There were no words that could assuage her pain, no sentiment capable of soothing the rawness of her loss. The trial had concluded, but her daughter would never return. That was a reality she refused to accept, an unyielding determination to keep Shantel's memory alive, even in the face of crushing injustice.

****

The days stretched into weeks, and the weeks morphed into months, with Sharon refusing to venture beyond the confines of her home. The once vibrant woman had become a mere shadow of her former self. Her friends, eager to lend their support during this trying time, reached out with invitations for outings, but Sharon waved them away. What was the point of indulging in frivolous pleasures when her daughter's life had been brutally extinguished, and the man responsible roamed free?

One evening, after dinner, Gary cautiously broached the topic. "Sharon, perhaps you should consider going out with the girls tonight," he suggested, his voice tinged with concern.

The suggestion hit Sharon like a slap in the face, and her anger flared. "How can you even suggest such a thing?" she snapped, her voice trembling with indignation. "After what happened to Shantel, how can you expect me to go out and pretend everything is fine? I don't understand how you can leave the house every morning as if nothing has changed."

Gary's eyes filled with sadness as he tried to reason with his wife. "I'm not suggesting that you go out and have a good time. I know you're devastated that Anthony wasn't convicted of Shantel's murder," he admitted. "But legally, without evidence or a motive, it was difficult to secure a conviction. We have to come to terms with that, as painful as it is. Staying cooped up inside isn't healthy for you. Your friends care about you and want to help."

"Don't you see?" Sharon's voice cracked with anguish. "If those women were truly my friends, they wouldn't pressure me to go out. They would understand the depth of my grief. They're mothers too; they should know how I feel. I'm not going out, and that's final!" With a resounding slam, she rose from the table, pushing her chair away.

Gary watched helplessly as Sharon stormed off to the bedroom, her sobs echoing through the house. This wasn't how he wanted the night to unfold. The strain in their relationship had been building, and he knew it would take more than a few minutes to resolve their differences.

He sighed as he cleared the table and washed the dishes, giving Sharon the solitude she desired. Each night, her cries reverberated through the hall, a painful reminder of their shared grief. He had hoped that suggesting she spend time with her friends would offer some solace, but he now understood why she had rejected the idea. Their friends were all mothers, and being in their company would only intensify the ache of Shantel's absence.

Finally, gathering his resolve, Gary ascended the stairs and approached the closed bedroom door. "Sharon?" he called out softly, his voice conveying his remorse.

"You can come in," Sharon replied, her voice choked with tears.

Gary entered the room and hurried to her side, enfolding her fragile form in his arms. "I'm so sorry," he whispered, his voice thick with regret. "I never should have said what I did."

Sharon sniffled, wiping her eyes. "You don't need to apologize. I understand why you said it. I haven't been much help since that day."

"We're both coping in our own ways," Gary admitted, his voice filled with understanding. "I've been going to the office early every morning to cry in private. I wanted to be strong for you, but inside, I'm shattered."

Sharon clung to him, her grip tightening. "I should have realized that," she murmured. "I can't believe I thought you weren't affected. But Gary, you didn't have to hide it from me."

"I know that now," Gary confessed, a tinge of shame coloring his words. "I don't know why I did it."

"I think I understand," Sharon replied, her voice filled with empathy. "We didn't receive the closure we needed when that monster escaped justice. Nothing can bring our daughter back, but seeing him behind bars would have been some form of recompense."

Gary nodded in agreement. "The endless days in court took their toll on us. It's a different experience being on the other side of the legal system, but I wish the outcome had been different. It's unbearable when the law fails to serve justice."

Sharon's voice trembled as she voiced her deepest fear. "Do you think he'll ever be caught?"

"In my years as a prosecutor, I've learned that criminals often make mistakes and eventually get caught," Gary assured her, his voice filled with a glimmer of hope. "We can only hope that he slips up and faces the consequences before he inflicts further harm on another family. Until then, we must try to live our lives. That's what Shantel would have wanted."

Reluctantly, Sharon acknowledged the truth in his words. The pain would never fully dissipate, but with time, they would have to find ways to heal and honor Shantel's memory. They would need to support each other and lean on their friends during this difficult journey. Perhaps, in time, Sharon would be ready to step out of the confines of her grief and embrace the world outside once again.

Together, they sat on the edge of the bed, holding each other tightly, finding solace in their shared pain. In that moment, they made a silent vow to continue fighting for justice, to cherish the memories of their daughter, and to rebuild their shattered lives, one step at a time.

∞ ∞ ∞

Chapter 5

Fifty years had elapsed since that fateful day, casting a haunting shadow over the house. The Riggs, who had courageously endured five years of residing there after Shantel's tragic murder, finally succumbed to the unbearable weight of the house's horrors. Anthony Welch, the killer still at large, loomed in their minds, suffusing their home with a palpable sense of dread. Sharon, plagued by perpetual fear, could never find solace within those walls, constantly worried that the murderer might return, seeking vengeance upon her and Gary. And so, one day, they made the decision to pack up their belongings and depart, yearning to leave the nightmare of the house behind them.

Now, on a different day, Damian and Sarah Atkinson arrived at the house, accompanied by their realtor, Thomas Porter. As they stepped onto the property, Thomas handed the couple the keys, a symbol of their newfound ownership.

Sarah, overcome with disbelief and excitement, tightly squeezed her husband's arm. "I can hardly believe this is happening," she exclaimed. "We finally have a place to call our own. Where's Alicia?" She scanned the surroundings, searching for their ten-year-old daughter.

"I think she's still in the car," Damian replied, his eyes darting around, unable to spot Alicia in the yard.

"I'll go get her. This move must be overwhelming for her," Sarah said empathetically, retracing her steps toward the car where Alicia sat in the backseat. "Alicia, wouldn't you like to see your new room?"

Alicia shook her head, her expression filled with uncertainty. "I don't understand why we had to move."

"We wanted to find a nicer house, one in a better neighborhood," Sarah explained. "Daddy and I already saw the house, and we know you're going to love it. Come inside, and you'll see."

Reluctantly, Alicia emerged from the car, clutching her mother's hand. She wasn't sure how she felt about this new house. Her parents had visited it one day while she stayed with her grandmother. When they returned, declaring their decision to move, Alicia couldn't help but feel a tinge of sadness, as she had grown attached to their previous home during the short year she spent there.

"Mom, where's my room?" Alicia tugged at Sarah's hand, her curiosity piqued.

"It would be best for her to go up to her room while I talk to you and your husband," Thomas interjected, addressing Sarah.

"Come with me, sweetie. I'll show you where your room is. You stay in there while Daddy and I sign the papers for the house," Sarah instructed, leading Alicia upstairs. She returned a few minutes later, joining Damian and Thomas downstairs. "What did you want to discuss with us?"

Damian, prompted by Thomas, began to explain. "Thomas was just telling us about the history of this home. Please, enlighten Sarah as well."

Thomas hesitated, reluctant to recount the grim tale but recognizing the necessity of divulging the truth. "I must admit, I'm not fond of recounting this story, but it's crucial that you know. I should have told you earlier, but there was a murder that occurred in the front yard of this house." He proceeded to recount the tragic details of Shantel's murder and the toll it took on her grieving parents, acknowledging that the killer had never been apprehended. "Now, I don't mean to instill fear or apprehension in you. There hasn't been another murder in this neighborhood since that night, and we can't even be certain if the murderer is still at large. I apologize for not informing you before you purchased the house."

Sarah exchanged a glance with Damian,

her newfound unease evident. However, Damian extended his hand, silently assuring her that everything would be alright.

"I believe it would be best to keep that story from Alicia," Damian suggested. "There's no need for her to know that a young girl lost her life here all those years ago."

"You're right," Sarah concurred, redirecting her attention to the realtor. "Is there anything else we should be aware of regarding this property?" She reproached herself for not asking these questions earlier.

Thomas reassured them, eager to salvage the sale. "Nothing as significant as that. This is West Mobile, one of the finest areas to live in. And you're acquiring this house for a steal. The airport is a few miles away, so the noise from planes might be bothersome initially, but I'm sure you'll acclimate to it in due time." Retrieving the papers from his briefcase, he continued, "All that remains is for both of you to sign the papers, and the house will officially be yours."

Sarah glanced at Damian, seeking affirmation before affixing her signature to the documents. "Are we absolutely certain about this?" Her internal doubts gnawed at her, but she was determined to overcome her reservations about the house now that she knew its dark history.

"Sarah, we've discussed this thoroughly," Damian reassured her. "This location is perfect for us, especially with Alicia."

"I know, but aren't you concerned about the fact that there's someone out there who once committed such a heinous act right outside our home?" Sarah voiced her lingering fears, unable to fully shake off the unsettling knowledge.

"Fifty years have passed," Damian reminded her gently. "And as Thomas mentioned, there haven't been any similar incidents since then. I truly believe it's safe for us to live here."

"Allow me to share a bit more about the area," Thomas interjected, sensing the couple's wavering resolve. He was determined not to lose the commission on this house. "Apart from that one tragic event, this house is ideal for a family."

Curiosity piqued, Sarah inquired, "In what way?"

"You mentioned that you moved here from an apartment in the city, correct?" Thomas prompted.

"Yes, and after adopting Alicia, we decided it would be best to raise her in a more rural setting," Sarah affirmed.

"Considering your husband's job is in the city, it makes perfect sense to settle in this area. The city district of Mobile is just minutes away. Without traffic, you can reach downtown within ten minutes. Simultaneously, you can provide your daughter with a country upbringing,"

Thomas explained, emphasizing the advantages of their chosen location. "Now," he tapped the papers with his pen, "what do you say?"

Damian, convinced by Thomas's reasoning, turned to Sarah. "He does make a compelling argument. It's a win-win situation for all of us."

Sarah, swayed by reason, couldn't deny the merits of the proposal. With a mix of apprehension and determination, she signed her name below Damian's on the papers. Thomas promptly retrieved the documents and stowed them in his briefcase.

"Thank you. I assure you, you won't regret this decision. May you enjoy many wonderful years in this house," Thomas stated, eager to conclude the transaction before any second thoughts arose. He swiftly departed, leaving the couple to embark on their new chapter, brimming with hope and trepidation.

****

As night fell, Sarah prepared herself for bed, feeling a mix of anticipation and unease about their recent move. She joined Damian in their bedroom, the dim glow of the bedside lamp casting a warm ambiance. The room was adorned with pictures of their family, capturing moments of joy and togetherness.

As Sarah entered, a furrowed brow revealed her inner turmoil. Damian, perceptive to her emotions, greeted her with a comforting smile.

"Sweetie, I know what's on your mind," he said, his voice filled with reassurance. "But there is nothing to worry about."

Her apprehension surfaced as she voiced her concerns. "How can you say that? You know what happens when people move into a house where a murder occurred."

Playfully dismissing her fears, Damian chuckled and rose from the bed, closing the distance between them. "You've seen one too many horror movies," he teased gently. With an affectionate touch, he continued, "We've been married for five years. When have I ever steered you wrong?"

Sarah's response was immediate and sincere. "Never."

Drawing her closer, Damian looked into her eyes, his voice filled with conviction. "Exactly. And I have a feeling this move was the best decision we've made. You'll see."

Sarah let out a weary sigh, her desire to believe in her husband's words evident. The primary motivation behind their move to the countryside was to provide Alicia with a better life. After experiencing the instability of foster homes, Sarah and Damian yearned for a quieter existence, a place where their daughter could thrive. However, Sarah remained unaware that their new home harbored a haunting history. If only Thomas had never mentioned the house's dark past, she thought, she could have blissfully lived her life here, oblivious to the tragic events that unfolded within those walls.

Seeking assurance, Sarah turned to Damian. "Do you really love this house?"

A smile danced upon Damian's lips as he responded, his voice brimming with enthusiasm. "I do. It's better than the cramped apartment we lived in during our time in the city. And the location is perfect. The car dealership isn't far. Moreover, I'll only be working on weekdays now. You know what that means," he said, his smile widening. "We'll be able to spend the weekends as a family."

Sarah's heart swelled with joy at the prospect of their newfound quality time together. In the city, Damian's demanding work schedule had left her feeling isolated in their apartment. She had attempted to find employment to occupy her time, but the bustling city had proven challenging. And when they adopted Alicia, Sarah made the decision to become a stay-at-home mom, dedicated to nurturing their daughter's well-being. Despite Alicia being of school age at the time of adoption, Sarah wanted to ensure she was always present, a constant source of love and support.

Damian noticed Sarah's silence, a hint of concern flickering in his eyes. "Feeling better about moving here?" he asked, his voice tinged with worry.

Sarah nodded, her lips curling into a faint smile. "I think I am. It might take me some time to adjust, but I do feel a sense of comfort settling in. Don't you sometimes wish Thomas never shared the story about this house?"

Damian's gaze softened as he contemplated her question. "Part of me does, but I also understand why he felt compelled to tell us. It could have caused problems if we found out later."

"And we both agree that we won't tell Alicia about this. Right?" Sarah sought reassurance, her voice carrying a note of protectiveness.

"Definitely," Damian affirmed, his eyes reflecting their shared commitment. "We want her to love this new place, not be burdened by fear."

Sarah leaned her head against Damian's chest, finding solace in his embrace. "It is a chilling thought, isn't it? To imagine what it must've been like for that poor girl's parents. They left her outside the house to play, only for her life to be tragically cut short."

Damian's head shook in disbelief as he contemplated the past. "It's hard to believe that even fifty years ago, it was dangerous to leave your kids unattended. Times have changed, thankfully. But one thing I know for certain is that we would never let anything like that happen to Alicia."

Sarah's voice quivered with determination as she spoke, her words carrying the weight of her unwavering devotion. "That's precisely why I chose to be a stay-at-home mother when we adopted her. I want her to feel safe with us, especially after everything she's been through in the foster homes."

A tender smile graced Damian's face as he responded, his voice filled with conviction. "We were meant to have Alicia in our lives, and I truly believe that."

With closed eyes, Sarah allowed herself to drift into a peaceful slumber, her mind consumed by thoughts of their journey of adopting Alicia and the unwavering love and protection she and Damian would provide. Yet, despite her best efforts, the specter of Shantel's murder lingered in her thoughts. Sarah reminded herself that the past was behind them, and no similar tragedy had occurred in their new town since then. With that reassurance, she surrendered to sleep, hopeful for the bright future that awaited them in their new home.

∞ ∞ ∞

Chapter 6

As the months went by, the Atkinson family settled into their new house, hoping for a smooth transition. Initially, everything appeared to be ordinary. Sarah and Damian were relieved to see that the move hadn't disrupted Alicia's life. She maintained contact with her friends from their previous neighborhood while forging new connections. Balancing her studies and leisure time, Alicia seemed to have mastered the art of navigating the pre-teen years effortlessly. Sarah couldn't help but laugh at her unnecessary worries.

However, as time passed, both Sarah and Damian noticed a shift in Alicia's behavior—one that seemed to be leading her down a different path. Damian, ever the optimist, attributed it to the typical behavior of a girl her age, dismissing it as a phase. Sarah, on the other hand, perceived it through a different lens.

One night, Sarah broached the topic with Damian, suggesting they make an appointment to speak with Alicia's principal.

Damian, however, had a different perspective. He believed that Alicia's behavior was just a normal part of adolescence and suggested that Sarah check her cell phone to gain insight into her life.

Sarah shook her head, rejecting the idea of invading their daughter's privacy. "Damian, I won't resort to snooping on our daughter," she said firmly. "Yes, I understand that girls her age go through changes, but this is different." She couldn't fathom how her husband failed to notice the stark difference in Alicia's behavior. Holding up a paper, she presented Alicia's latest math test —a failing grade. "Explain this to me. She has been a straight-A student since she started school, and now she's failing."

Damian took the papers, his expression filled with concern. He understood why Sarah was apprehensive. Alicia had been an exemplary student, consistently praised by her teachers since they arrived at this new school. The sudden decline in her academic performance was puzzling.

"What do you think we should do?" Damian asked, sharing his wife's worry.

Sarah sighed, feeling helpless. "I don't know. I've been trying to come up with something, but how do we approach her about this without overwhelming her?"

Before Damian could respond, the front door swung open, and Alicia walked in, immediately sensing the tension in the room.

"What?" Alicia snapped, noticing her parents' intense gazes fixed upon her.

"Alicia, come here. We need to talk," Sarah said, maintaining a calm tone.

"Can this wait? I have things to do," Alicia retorted, walking past them and heading toward the stairs.

"Get back here right now," Damian demanded. "You don't ignore your mother. We have something serious to discuss."

Reluctantly, Alicia rolled her eyes and threw her backpack onto the floor. She returned to the kitchen table, crossing her arms defiantly. "What do you want?"

Sarah took a deep breath, her voice steady. "Is there something happening at school that you're not telling us?"

"It's just school. What more is there to say?" Alicia replied dismissively.

"Alicia, your teachers gave me these test papers the other day. They're concerned because your grades have suddenly plummeted. I know this isn't like you," Sarah explained, concern etched on her face.

Alicia's frustration boiled over, and her words cut deep. "And how do you know who I am? You're not my real parents!" she snapped. "I don't have to stay here and listen to this. I'm out of here!" Abruptly, she stormed off to her bedroom, slamming the door shut behind her.

Sarah let out a weary sigh, exchanging a glance with Damian. "Now what?"

"I wish I had an answer. One thing I know is that this isn't the Alicia we know. Yes, we've only had her for a year, but she has never shown any signs of hostility before," Damian replied, his voice laced with worry.

Sarah contemplated Alicia's outburst, her mind grappling with the possibility that Alicia's words held a grain of truth. "What if she's right? What if we don't truly know the real Alicia because we adopted her?" she pondered aloud.

"Sarah, all we can do now is hope that this is just a phase she's going through—a temporary deviation from her true self. We have to believe that she will find her way back to us," Damian reassured, longing for their daughter's return to the loving girl they had welcomed into their family.

****

As the weeks went by, Sarah and Damian couldn't shake off their growing concern for Alicia. Her transformation went beyond just a change in style. The atmosphere in their house shifted, as if cloaked in a heavy veil of darkness. Alicia's room became a fortress, an impenetrable sanctuary where she sought solace. The walls, once adorned with bright posters and colorful artwork, now stood barren and bare, mirroring the emptiness that had settled within their daughter.

Sarah's heart sank when she accompanied Alicia to the mall, hoping for a glimpse of normalcy. But instead, they ventured into stores filled with shadowy attire. The vibrant hues that once graced Alicia's wardrobe were replaced by an array of black dresses and boots. The transformation was jarring, as if her daughter had stepped into an alternate reality, a world Sarah struggled to comprehend.

Alicia's physical appearance mirrored the darkness that had enveloped her spirit. The ponytail that once bounced with her every step was replaced by straight hair cascading down her face, concealing her eyes from the world. The sparkle in her gaze, once filled with curiosity and wonder, had dimmed, veiled by an impenetrable sadness.

Days turned into weeks, and Alicia's withdrawal from the world intensified. Her room became a fortress of solitude, a sanctuary where she sought refuge from the outside world. She isolated herself, retreating into her cocoon the moment she stepped through the front door. Even mealtimes became solitary affairs, with plates of food delivered to her room, an attempt to nourish her body while her soul remained distant.

One Saturday afternoon, Sarah's concern reached a tipping point. She couldn't bear to witness her daughter's self-imposed exile any longer. Desperate for a solution, she turned to Damian for support. "We have to do something," she pleaded, her voice tinged with worry. "This isn't healthy for her. She should be out with friends, experiencing the joy of her youth."

Damian nodded, his own heart heavy with concern. "Have you tried talking to her? Maybe she needs to know we're here for her."

"I've tried," Sarah admitted, her voice tinged with frustration. "But she shuts us out. She's made it clear that she wants to stay in her room."

As if on cue, the doorbell rang, interrupting their conversation. Damian answered the door, and to their surprise, Alicia's friends, Emily and Sophia, stood on the other side. Their presence was a glimmer of hope, a lifeline in the darkness.

"Emily! Sophia!" Damian greeted them warmly. "Please, come in."

"Thank you, Mr. Atkinson," Emily said, her voice filled with genuine concern. "Sophia and I were on our way to the park, and we thought maybe Alicia would like to join us."

"We've noticed she's been a little down lately," Sophia added. "We hoped some time outside would help lift her spirits."

Sarah's face brightened with gratitude. "That's a wonderful idea. Let me go and see if she's willing to come."

Sarah made her way upstairs, her footsteps heavy with anticipation. She knocked softly on Alicia's door, her heart pounding in her chest. "Alicia, it's me," she called out gently.

"What?" Alicia's voice dripped with annoyance, a shield meant to keep the world at bay.

"Emily and Sophia are here. They want to know if you'd like to go to the park with them," Sarah said, her voice filled with hope.

Alicia's response was immediate, laced with frustration. "No. I already told you. I don't want to leave my room."

Sarah's heart sank, but she refused to give

up. "Alicia, you shouldn't be cooped up inside on a beautiful Saturday. It'll do you good to get some fresh air."

"I said I don't want to go! CAN'T YOU JUST LEAVE ME ALONE?" Alicia's voice cracked with desperation, the pain she felt bleeding through her words.

Resigned, Sarah made her way back downstairs, her shoulders slumped. "Girls, thank you for thinking of Alicia, but she's not in the mood to go to the park today."

"We understand, Mrs. Atkinson," Emily said, her voice filled with empathy. "We hope she feels better soon."

The couple exchanged worried glances, their hearts heavy with the weight of their daughter's anguish. The girl upstairs, hidden behind closed doors, was a mere shadow of the vibrant soul they had welcomed into their lives. Desperation mingled with love as they grappled with the challenge of reaching out to the daughter who seemed lost within herself.

****

Sarah's heart sank as she rummaged through Alicia's backpack, her fingers brushing against the crumpled invitation to Skye's birthday party. Determined to confront her daughter and unravel the mystery behind her recent behavior, she bypassed the usual polite knock and entered Alicia's room unannounced. Startled, Alicia jolted upright in her bed.

"Mom!" she exclaimed, a mix of surprise and frustration in her voice.

"Alicia, we need to talk," Sarah's tone remained firm, her eyes searching for answers.

"Couldn't it wait?" Alicia pleaded, her voice tinged with weariness.

"When, Alicia? When will we have a chance to talk? You've barricaded yourself in this room, isolating yourself from the world. You only leave for school and retreat straight back here when you return. Now, explain why I found this in your backpack?" Sarah handed over the birthday invitation, her eyes fixed on Alicia's face.

Alicia shrugged, a nonchalant gesture that belied the significance of her actions. "I didn't feel like going."

"Skye is your best friend, Alicia. Why wouldn't you want to attend her party?" Sarah pressed, her concern deepening.

"Mom, there's no particular reason. I just don't feel like it. Can't I stay home? Is that so wrong?" Alicia's voice held a hint of defiance.

"Alicia, it's not just about missing a party. It's

everything that's been happening in the past few months. You've changed," Sarah's voice trembled with a mixture of worry and frustration.

"And?" Alicia's response dripped with indifference. She failed to grasp the magnitude of her transformation. "Isn't change a normal part of life?"

"Not like this, Alicia. Your behavior goes beyond typical teenage mood swings. You're barely eating, avoiding family meals, and your teachers have expressed concern about your eating habits at school. They mentioned you sit alone, barely touching your food," Sarah revealed, her voice heavy with concern.

"So now you're discussing me with my teachers behind my back?" Alicia retorted, her anger simmering beneath the surface.

"They reach out to me because they care about you," Sarah sighed, her voice tinged with sadness. "We all care about you."

"There's nothing to worry about. That's what you want to hear, right? There's nothing wrong. You've only known me for a year. You don't know what I was like before you adopted me. If you don't mind, I'd like to be alone," Alicia's voice cracked with a mix of frustration and pain.

Sarah realized that pushing further would only drive a bigger wedge between them. She reluctantly retreated from Alicia's room, her heart heavy with a sense of helplessness. Descending the stairs, she found Damian in the kitchen, his concerned gaze meeting hers.

"What happened?" Damian inquired, sensing the weight of the situation.

"I don't know what to do anymore," Sarah admitted, sinking into a chair at the kitchen table. "I confronted her about the birthday invitation, and she brushed it off like it was nothing. But it's more than that, Damian. It's everything—her eating habits, her withdrawal from everything. I can't shake this feeling that there's something deeper going on."

Damian sat beside her, his presence offering solace. "I was hoping it was just a passing phase, but it seems more serious than we thought."

"I had the same hope, but it's clear now that it's not just a phase," Sarah replied, her voice laced with worry. "The question is, what do we do next for Alicia?"

"Let's schedule a meeting with her teacher. We can both take time off work and address our concerns together," Damian suggested, his voice filled with determination.

"That's a good idea. I'll call the school on Monday and arrange a meeting," Sarah agreed, finding a glimmer of hope in Damian's support.

Damian wrapped his arm around Sarah's shoulders, offering comfort and reassurance. "We'll find out what's going on, Sarah. We'll get to the bottom of this and get Alicia the help she needs."

As they clung to each other, their love for Alicia and their determination to guide her through this dark period became the driving force that propelled them forward, ready to face the challenges that lay ahead.

∞ ∞ ∞

Chapter 7

Sarah made an appointment for her and Damian to meet with Alicia's teacher, Charles Sanders, later that week. She and her husband sat in the classroom, waiting for the teacher to come back from dropping the class off for dismissal, her leg nervously shaking. Damian was doing all he could to calm his wife down, but he was also worried about what they were going to find out about their daughter. She wasn't the same girl they adopted a year ago and all he wanted was for them to get their daughter back.

"Sarah, calm down sweetie," he whispered in her ear. "We're here because we want to help Alicia. Don't we want to get help for her?"

"Yes, of course, we do." Sarah took a deep breath and exhaled, calming down.

"Mr. and Mrs. Atkinson, sorry to keep you waiting," the teacher walked in. "It's great to see the two of you again," he shook their hands. The first time they met with Charles was when they enrolled Alicia into the school and they wanted to tell him, as well as her other teachers, about her childhood. Back then, she was a pleasure to have in a class and there was no need for other meetings.

"Mr. Sanders, I am so sorry to bother you. I'm sure you have to be busy with work you have to do for the class," Sarah said.

"I'm never too busy to talk to parents about their kids. Especially when it's something serious like what is happening with Alicia."

"Has it gotten worse for her at school? We've noticed at home she doesn't come out of her room anymore. Not even to eat. At first, my wife and I thought it was because she was trying to adjust to going to a new school. If you remember what we told you when she started coming here, she was passed around from foster homes. It made sense that finally settling down was going to take time for her, but we don't know what to do anymore," Damian said.

"I understand your concern and I have to say, myself, as well as Alicia's other teachers, are concerned about the change in her behavior. At first, she was always helpful in the classroom. I could always rely on her to help me in the classroom. And she was passing all her tests. At lunch and recess, she always hung out with Skye and a bunch of other friends"

"And now?" Sarah asked, though she already knew the answer. Alicia didn't want to spend time with anyone.

"That's what concerns me the most," Charles said. "Now, she doesn't want to talk to anyone in the class. At lunch, she always hides in the corner. She doesn't even get lunch anymore. That's when I started to realize it's become serious."

"What do you suggest we should do? I have tried talking to her, but she keeps kicking me out of her room when I do," Sarah said. "She says this is who she really is and we don't know her since she was adopted. That doesn't sit well with me because I thought we would've picked up on behavior like this before."

"And you said it was a year ago you adopted her?" Charles asked.

"Yes. She was only at the school for a year, but she made friends. Two of them stopped by not too long ago, asking if she would've liked to hang out with them, but she said no. I found that odd because she always loved spending time with them," Sarah added.

"What are the names of those friends? I think I may have a feeling of what is going on," the teacher said.

"Really?" Sarah was hopeful they were finally onto something. Any progress would be helpful as to what they should do next.

"I'm wondering if she's starting to miss her friends from the old school. That could explain the sudden change in her behavior."

Sarah turned to her husband and shrugged. What if it was something as simple as her missing her two best friends from the old school? "Their names are Emily and Sophia."

Charles's face fell and Alicia's parents could tell this wasn't good news. "Let me guess. None of those names ring a bell, do they?" Damian asked.

"Sorry, they don't. She's been talking about a friend named Shantel," the teacher informed them.

"Shantel?" Sarah repeated the name. "I never heard that name mentioned before." She turned to her husband. "Have you?"

He shook his head. "Who's this Shantel? Is it a girl from another class?"

"That's the thing. I've asked the principal if there's a student with that name, but there's no Shantel in this school."

This came as a shock to Sarah and Damian. They never heard Alicia mention this name at home and they didn't know where she got it from.

"Mr. Sanders, is she talking to this person at school?" Sarah asked.

"That's just it, none of us have seen her with anyone. The teachers on lunch duty say she's always alone. When she first came here, she was always with Skye. I have spoken to Skye and she said she doesn't know what's wrong with Alicia. She said the last time Alicia spoke to her was three weeks ago and then she just stopped."

"And she refused to go to Skye's birthday party this past weekend," Sarah brought up. "I tried to get her to go, but she said no."

Charles attentively listened to Sarah as she explained Alicia's sudden change in behavior and never coming out of her room. The more he was told about his student, it was beginning to add up to what he witnessed in his classroom.

"I've seen changes in students, especially at this age. They always want to fit in with their friends, so they start failing tests. Acting too cool. I've seen it all before. But something is going on with Alicia that doesn't feel right."

"Mr. Sanders, we're looking for any help we can get with her. I can't stand to see her locking herself in her room every day," Sarah started to cry. "I know when we first moved here, she wasn't happy. But then I saw the change in her and she looked like she was enjoying herself in this town. I thought things were starting to go well when she made friends with Skye."

"Mrs. Atkinson, I want to do whatever it is we can to get to the bottom of this. Before I did anything about this, I wanted to run it by the two of you first. I think maybe it would be a good idea for Alicia to see the school counselor."

"Is this something my husband and I could discuss first?" Sarah asked. She didn't have anything against Alicia going to a counselor, but she thought something this serious would be better if they did it as a family.

"Yes, of course. But I must warn you Mr. and Mrs. Atkinson, I wouldn't take too long to make a decision. There was another reason why I wanted to meet with the two of you today. You see, it's been brought to my attention that Alicia has threatened to harm some of the students and teachers."

Sarah and Damian tried to remain calm hearing this news. Why didn't the teacher mention this at the beginning of the meeting instead of waiting this long? Their daughter was threatening students and they couldn't believe this was the same girl they adopted a year ago.

"And what did you do when she threatened these students?" Damian asked.

"Well, she was sent to the principal's office. Unfortunately, once she got there, she didn't speak to the principal either. And they sent her back to school."

"Mr. Sanders, thank you for bringing this to our attention. We will discuss this at home and see what the next step is for us to take," Sarah said.

Sarah and Damian walked out of the school and sat in their car for a few minutes before driving home. What they were just told was a lot to take in and neither were in the mood to drive in their current state.

"He is right about one thing, Alicia needs help," Damian said. "It's not normal for her to threaten students and teachers."

"I know. I know." Sarah sighed. "But what if we found a counselor that we can see as a family. I don't know how I feel about her going to a counselor in school without us present. I want this to be something we do together. We need to find out what is going on with her," she started to cry. "I want our daughter back."

Damien never saw his wife a mess before and he pulled her into a tight embrace, rubbing her back as she cried on his shoulder. "I know how you feel. I keep feeling useless that we aren't getting through to her. But we will. I agree with you that we should go to family counseling."

Sarah pulled away from her husband and dried her eyes. "So, we agree with this? That we look for a counselor we can all see together?"

"I don't see any other option for us," Damian said. "I am willing to do whatever we can to get the old Alicia back. Now, before we go home, let's discuss something else. This Shantel girl she's been talking about."

"I've never heard that name before in my life," Sarah said. "Sky was her only friend here and there was no Shantel she hung out with at her old school."

"That's what I found odd too. I know she's gotten quiet, but I'm sure we would've heard this name before," Damian said.

Sarah agreed. Even if Alicia was being quiet, she knew that this name would've been mentioned before. "When we get home, let's see if she tells us anything about Shantel."

"Or wait until we hear her mention the name," Damian said. "You and I both know she won't willingly give us information on this friend."

"You're right. We have to be more alert with what she's saying and doing," Sarah said. Alicia already hated that the teachers were calling Sarah with news on her behavior, Sarah didn't even want to think of what she would do if she found out they went to see her teacher.

$\infty \infty \infty$

Chapter 8

Sarah's heart pounded anxiously as she stood in the kitchen, her worry etched on her face. The weight of the recent meeting with Alicia's teacher lingered heavily, casting a shadow of fear over each passing day. The thought of receiving a phone call from the school, informing her that Alicia had harmed someone, haunted Sarah's thoughts. Doubts began to gnaw at her, questioning their decision to wait and see if things worsened before seeking professional help. What if they had underestimated the urgency of the situation? What if Alicia's actions escalated, resulting in harm to herself or others?

"Are you sure this will work?" Sarah's voice quivered with uncertainty as she turned to Damian on that fateful Saturday morning.

With a reassuring tone, Damian replied, his voice laced with determination, "Trust me, this is the only way we'll find out what's going on. I understand your concerns, Sarah. I share them too. But it's Saturday, and we know Alicia is likely to remain secluded in her room. If we keep a watchful eye and listen closely as we pass by, we may catch her mentioning Shantel."

To their astonishment, Alicia descended the stairs, her presence an unexpected sight. Sarah's eyes widened in surprise as she struggled to find her voice, "Alicia, is everything alright?"

Alicia responded calmly, almost nonchalantly, "Yes, everything is fine. I'm going to go outside and play with Shantel," before promptly leaving the house.

Sarah and Damian exchanged bewildered glances, struggling to process what they had just witnessed. Sarah's voice trembled with a mix of confusion and concern, "Did she just say, Shantel?"

Damian pondered the possibility, questioning, "She did. Could it be that Shantel is someone she met in the neighborhood?"

"It's possible," Sarah mused. "We don't know if she made any new friends on those days she went out with her peers. Perhaps Shantel attends a different school, which is why her teacher didn't recognize the name."

Damian let out a nervous chuckle, attempting to ease the tension. "You might be onto something. Let's take a look outside and see who this Shantel is."

Peering through the window, Sarah and Damian were taken aback by the sight that greeted them. Alicia sat alone on the front lawn, her actions perplexing. Damian shrugged, a puzzled expression on his face, "Damian, what is she doing?"

Observing Alicia's behavior, Sarah grabbed her coat, her curiosity piqued. She ventured outside, her mind entertaining thoughts of a game of hide and seek between the two girls. However, as she approached her daughter, Sarah's ears caught Alicia's words, and her heart sank.

"I wish they would just leave me alone," Alicia's voice carried a mixture of frustration and desperation. "I don't know why it's anyone's business how I'm acting. I know I promised not to mention your name to anyone, but I couldn't help it. They were all breathing down my neck, I had to tell them. No, don't worry. I didn't tell them who you really were. I said you were a friend of mine."

Unable to bear the weight of Alicia's words, Sarah's emotions surged, and she hurriedly retreated indoors, slamming the door shut behind her.

Concern etched on his face, Damian approached his distressed wife. "What's wrong?" he inquired, seeking solace in understanding.

Sarah, her voice trembling with a mixture of

shock and disbelief, managed to utter, "I... I don't know. When I went outside, hoping to find Alicia playing with Shantel, there was no one there. And then I heard Alicia speaking to someone who wasn't there."

Damian's mind processed the information, attempting to make sense of the situation. "Do you mean like an imaginary friend?"

Sarah's realization was palpable as she exclaimed, "Yes! That's it. I think Shantel is an imaginary friend she has. It would explain everything that's been happening." Relief began to wash over her, finally finding a semblance of understanding amidst the chaos. "Now, the question is, what do we do about this?"

Deep in thought, Damian reflected on his own childhood experiences. "She's ten. Remember what it was like at that age? I had an imaginary friend too."

Curiosity piqued, Sarah inquired about his parents' approach to the situation. Damian's voice held a touch of nostalgia as he recounted, "They played along with it. Pretended my imaginary friend was real. They let me talk about him all the time. And one day, he simply disappeared when I grew bored of him."

Sarah nodded, a glimmer of hope in her eyes. "That could work. There could be numerous reasons why Alicia created this imaginary friend. I don't see any harm in her having this friend. And if it does become more concerning, we can bring it up with her therapist."

****

Sarah placed her trust in her husband's judgment, convinced that he understood the situation and knew what was best for Alicia. Together, they fostered their daughter's friendship with Shantel, encouraging her to spend weekends outdoors with her imaginary companion. However, Sarah couldn't help but feel a sense of unease when Alicia chose to play with Shantel outside, as she worried about the judgmental stares and whispers from the townsfolk. The rumors surrounding Alicia's disruptive behavior at school only added to Sarah's concerns, and she dreaded the possibility of onlookers witnessing her daughter engaging in conversations with an unseen presence.

One afternoon, as Alicia returned from school, Sarah heard the front door close with a soft click. Aware of her daughter's unpredictable moods, she approached their conversation with caution, hoping for a glimpse into Alicia's day.

"Hey, Alicia, how was school today?" Sarah's voice carried a gentle tone, her curiosity piqued.

Alicia shrugged nonchalantly, giving little

away. "It was fine. Oh, I played with Shantel at lunch."

Sarah's ears perked up at the mention of Shantel's name. She remembered her agreement with Damian to go along with Alicia's imaginary friend, but the fact that Shantel had made an appearance at school raised new concerns. "Shantel? She was at school today?" Sarah tried to maintain her composure, unsure of how deeply Alicia had immersed herself in this fantasy.

Alicia nodded, a mischievous smile gracing her lips. "Yep, she goes to my school. She prefers staying quiet, so people tend to forget she exists." With that, Alicia excused herself, retreating to her room with Shantel in tow.

Sarah's worry intensified, prompting her to reach for her phone. She knew it was time to seek professional help for Alicia's sake, and she dialed the counselor's number they had found.

"Hello, Jesse Lyon speaking. How may I help you?" The counselor's warm voice greeted Sarah on the other end.

"Mr. Lyon, this is Sarah Atkinson," she replied, her voice tinged with anxiety.

"Ah, Sarah. It's a pleasure to hear from you. How are things going with Alicia?" Mr. Lyon's calm demeanor provided a glimmer of comfort.

Sarah struggled to find the right words, her concern palpable. "I... I don't know how to explain it. We agreed with my husband to play along with the imaginary friend idea, but now I'm scared. Alicia mentioned spending her entire school day with this friend, and she even said that Shantel would be joining us for dinner. I'm afraid she's starting to believe Shantel is real."

Mr. Lyon's reassuring tone offered solace in the midst of Sarah's distress. "Mrs. Atkinson, take a deep breath and try to calm down. While I haven't had the opportunity to speak with Alicia yet, based on what you and your husband have shared about her difficult childhood, this imaginary friend may be a source of comfort for her. Though it seems unsettling to you right now, remember that Alicia created this friend as a means of coping. Please keep me informed of any developments until I have a chance to meet with her. In the meantime, you and your husband are doing the right thing by allowing her to express herself and talk about Shantel."

"Thank you, Doctor Lyon," Sarah responded, her voice laced with gratitude. With renewed determination, she made a mental note to discuss the day's events with Damian when he returned home. They would face this challenge together, reminding themselves that Alicia's behavior was likely a passing phase, a manifestation of her need for solace in a difficult world.

****

Restless and anxious, Sarah found herself at a loss as she awaited Damian's return from work. With limited options, she ventured into Alicia's room, hoping to catch a glimpse of her daughter conversing with Shantel. However, the door remained closed, concealing whatever was transpiring within.

A flicker of relief washed over Sarah as the sound of the front door opening reached her ears. She hurried downstairs, eager to embrace Damian. "Damian," she exclaimed, wrapping her arms around him.

"I'm glad to be home," he replied, his smile fading as he sensed his wife's distress. "What's wrong?"

"I had to call Doctor Lyon. I was worried when Alicia returned from school," Sarah explained, recounting the story of Alicia's friendship with Shantel and her conversation with the counselor.

Damian furrowed his brow, contemplating their course of action. "So, we just pretend like it's nothing?"

"That's what the doctor advised. We continue doing what we've been doing, acting as if Shantel is real. He believes that Alicia may be clinging to this imaginary friend for comfort, given everything she's been through. It's just... troubling to see her forsaking her real friends for an imaginary one," Sarah confessed, seeking solace in Damian's embrace.

"Let's follow the doctor's advice. We'll treat it as if it's nothing out of the ordinary. He knows better than us. All we can do is be there for Alicia," Damian suggested, holding his wife tightly.

"Alright, that's what we'll do," Sarah agreed, nodding resolutely. "Dinner is almost ready," she added, reluctantly releasing herself from Damian's embrace. A faint smile formed on her lips as she added, "And I should warn you, Shantel will be joining us for dinner."

"Oh, really?" Damian stifled a laugh, aware of the gravity of the situation. They needed to maintain a delicate balance, finding moments of levity amidst the seriousness of Alicia's situation.

"That's what Alicia told me. She's upstairs with Shantel right now," Sarah replied, her voice tinged with a mixture of concern and curiosity.

"Have you tried listening in on them in the bedroom?" Damian inquired, his curiosity mirroring Sarah's.

"I'm one step ahead of you. I did try to listen, but it was quiet. Who knows what's happening in there," Sarah replied, shrugging her shoulders.

"Well, I suppose we'll find out during dinner. You have to admit, it's the first time in weeks that she's joined us," Damian pointed out, hoping to find a glimmer of positivity in the situation.

Sarah's mind was consumed by Alicia's interactions with her imaginary friend, making it difficult for her to perceive the silver lining Damian had pointed out. She hadn't realized that Alicia's absence from the dinner table had coincided with Shantel's arrival. Moreover, Alicia had been skipping breakfast, claiming she would eat on her way to school—an excuse Sarah knew to be false, as her daughter's weight loss was becoming increasingly apparent.

"I'll freshen up and change for dinner," Damian mentioned, planting a tender kiss on his wife's forehead. "Take a deep breath and try to calm down. Everything will work out."

"I know it will," Sarah responded, her voice laced with newfound conviction. She believed in her husband's reassurances, berating herself for initially making a big fuss over the situation. After all, she hadn't received any more complaints from the teachers about Alicia's disruptive behavior, which was a positive sign. Shantel might be an imaginary friend, but Sarah couldn't deny the positive influence this entity seemed to have on her daughter. All she and Damian could do was offer unwavering support during this challenging time. And if this turned out to be a passing phase, all the better.

∞ ∞ ∞

Chapter 9

Alicia's behavior continued to undergo a disconcerting transformation as each passing day brought forth new concerns for Sarah and Damian. The frequency of meetings with Mr. Sanders, the school principal, had skyrocketed, reaching an astonishing count of over twenty times within the last three months alone. Today, Sarah and Damian found themselves once again summoned to his classroom after school, their hearts heavy with foreboding. The nature of these encounters had taken on an increasingly eerie quality, as each meeting unveiled a fresh revelation about their daughter's unsettling conduct within the school walls. The Alicia they had lovingly welcomed into their lives was slipping further away with every passing moment.

As the door creaked open, Mr. Sanders entered the room, his gaze filled with a mixture of empathy and concern. He offered a faint smile in greeting, though it failed to mask the gravity of the situation. "I'm sorry to have to call you in again so soon after our last meeting," he began, his voice laced with regret.

"There's no need to apologize," Damian responded, his voice tinged with worry. "We appreciate your efforts in keeping us updated on Alicia's school life. What has happened this time?"

Mr. Sanders hesitated for a moment, his eyes flickering with a hint of apprehension. "Before I delve into the recent events, I must ask if you've noticed any unusual behavior from Alicia at home?"

Sarah knew that the truth about Shantel, Alicia's imaginary friend, could no longer be concealed from the teacher. It was time to lay bare the catalyst behind their daughter's transformation. "Has she been mentioning Shantel?" she inquired, her voice tinged with a mix of resignation and concern.

Mr. Sanders nodded solemnly. "Indeed, she has. In fact, that's precisely why I requested this meeting today. Alicia spoke of Shantel in a manner that suggested Shantel was physically present, as if she were a real person. But, as I informed you several months ago, there is no one named Shantel enrolled in our school."

"There's a reason you're unaware of Shantel's existence," Sarah confessed, her voice filled with a touch of sorrow. She proceeded to explain the revelation they had made about Shantel being an imaginary companion. "We've sought the guidance of a counselor, who attempted to engage with Alicia, but she refuses to communicate with him. Instead, Damian and I have found ourselves taking part in these sessions. Yet, the counselor keeps imparting the same advice."

Curiosity etched across Mr. Sanders' face as he leaned forward, eager to hear more. "And what advice might that be?" he inquired.

Sarah cast a meaningful glance at her husband, silently urging him to continue. Damian, torn between his growing conviction and his wife's reservations, took a deep breath and began to share his thoughts. "The counselor suggested that we play along with Alicia's phase of having an imaginary friend. We initially believed it was the right course of action. We hoped that by acknowledging Shantel's presence as real, Alicia would eventually let go of her. Unfortunately, all it seems to have done is solidify Alicia's belief that Shantel is indeed a tangible presence in her life."

As Damian spoke, Mr. Sanders diligently transcribed their words, his pen dancing across the paper, etching out a record of their concerns. "I understand," he responded, his tone grave. "I will discuss this matter with Mr. Taylor Brailey, our school counselor. Perhaps he can offer more insight or help us determine the next steps to take."

Sarah interjected, her voice laced with a mix of anxiety and urgency. "What should we do in the meantime?"

Mr. Sanders leaned back in his chair, his eyes contemplating the gravity of the situation. "Keep a watchful eye on Alicia and make note of any notable changes in her behavior. These observations will prove invaluable when discussing the matter with Mr. Brailey. Meanwhile, while she's here at school, we will closely monitor Alicia's interactions and observe how far this manifestation of Shantel extends."

"We will do as you suggest, Mr. Sanders. Thank you once again for your unwavering dedication to Alicia's well-being," Sarah expressed her gratitude, her voice infused with both relief and concern.

The room fell into a brief silence, the weight of uncertainty hanging in the air. As Sarah and Damian left the classroom, they couldn't help but feel the weight of their daughter's diminishing connection to reality, and the daunting road that lay ahead in their quest to restore her to herself.

****

Damian guided the car into their garage, the engine's hum fading into silence as they sat together, enveloped in a heavy silence. The weight of their concerns pressed upon them, prompting a cautious discussion about their impending encounter with Alicia once they stepped foot inside their home.

"We need to approach her delicately," Damian suggested, his voice laced with a trace of worry. "Whenever we broach the subject of her behavior, she becomes defensive."

Sarah nodded in agreement, her expression mirroring her husband's concern. "You're right. But we can't let her actions go unchecked. Her mistreatment of both students and teachers is a serious matter."

"Let's assess the situation once we're inside," Damian proposed. "We do need to inform her about our meeting with Mr. Bailey."

Sarah sighed, her apprehension evident. "I know we have to, but it won't be well-received by Alicia," she confessed before stepping out of the car.

The Atkinsons entered their house to find Alicia perched on the living room couch. The television remained dormant, its silence overshadowed by the sound of Alicia engaging in conversation with Shantel.

"Alicia, why don't you turn on the TV and watch something?" Sarah suggested, her voice laced with a gentle tone.

"Shantel doesn't care for any of the shows currently airing. And honestly, she's right. Have you seen the quality of programs these days?" Alicia retorted, her gaze shifting towards her parents. "Where were you? Mom is usually here when I come home from school."

"Your teacher, Mr. Sanders, requested a meeting with us," Sarah explained.

"What was it about?" Alicia snapped, her tone laced with defiance.

"Alicia," Damian interjected, making his way to the couch and taking a seat beside her. "We need to have a conversation."

"No, we don't," Alicia retorted sharply, rising from the couch. "Whatever Mr. Sanders had to say about me isn't true. I can't understand why he feels the need to pry into my business! I won't stand here and endure this! I'm going upstairs with Shantel!" With that, she stormed off to her room.

"Well, that went as expected," Damian sighed, his voice filled with a tinge of disappointment.

"How do we even attempt to communicate with her when she refuses to listen?" Sarah pondered, a hint of desperation creeping into her voice.

"I'm running out of ideas," Damian admitted, his frustration palpable. "And it's clear that humoring her imaginary friend concept isn't yielding positive results. Is there anything else we can do?"

"Hopefully, Mr. Bailey will be able to reach her," Sarah mused, her gaze drifting downward. "All we want is to get to the bottom of this. Who is Shantel, and how did Alicia conjure her up?"

Damian approached his wife, his footsteps heavy with resolve. "It may take time, but we'll find a resolution. We'll get to the bottom of this, I promise."

Sarah's eyes met his, the weight of uncertainty etched on her face. "I truly hope so," she confessed softly, her gaze lingering on the ground below, as if seeking solace in the floor's embrace.

****

The days dragged on, each one marked by Alicia's escalating misbehavior at school. Sarah, growing increasingly concerned for her daughter's safety, made the decision to personally pick her up after dismissal, a choice met with fierce opposition from Alicia. Every afternoon, Sarah pulled into the school parking lot, only to be greeted by Alicia's stormy entrance into the car, the door slamming shut with a resounding thud. Alicia sought to express her vehement disapproval of being picked up, employing every means at her disposal. Her walks home had previously been a time for her to engage in conversations with Shantel, but now she was confined to the car with her mother.

"This is utterly unbelievable," Alicia huffed, crossing her arms defiantly as she flung herself into the backseat.

"Why don't you come sit in the front?" Sarah suggested calmly, choosing to ignore her daughter's hostile demeanor.

"I'd rather not sit next to you," Alicia retorted sharply.

"Why not? We can chat on the way home," Sarah persisted, maintaining her composure.

"About what, mother?" Alicia's glare bore into Sarah's eyes. "I know you keep in touch with Mr. Sanders and that absurd counselor he insists I see. I'm sure they'll report to you about my day, as if they know me better than I know myself." There was a brief moment of silence before Alicia continued. "You're right, Shantel. I shouldn't have to answer to anyone about my day."

Sarah attempted to remain calm, but her composure wavered when Alicia mentioned Shantel. She had hoped that driving Alicia home would distract her from her imaginary friend.

"Well, are we going to drive, or are we going to linger here until it's time to return tomorrow?" Alicia impatiently demanded.

"I'm going," Sarah started the car, her voice tinged with a hint of resignation. "Alicia, before we head home, there's one thing I'd like to ask. Please don't talk about Shantel when it's just the two of us."

"I'm not talking about Shantel. I'm talking to her," Alicia snapped back. "Maybe you should mind your own business and simply drive. Stop eavesdropping on my conversations with my friend."

"Alicia, look, I know there must be a reason why you've created Shantel, but it's becoming increasingly difficult for me to accept this imaginary friend of yours, especially when you're conversing with her in public," Sarah explained, her voice laden with concern.

"I knew it." Alicia's gaze turned sinister, her eyes locking onto her mother's. "This is all about how people will perceive you, isn't it? Oh, little miss perfect can't risk tarnishing her reputation with the other mothers here. Poor Sarah Atkinson, she adopted a peculiar daughter, didn't she? One who talks to what society deems an imaginary friend. Well, let me tell you one thing. Shantel is real, and she's the only person who truly listens to me. Now, just drive us home," Alicia demanded, her tone filled with defiance.

Sarah could no longer bear the weight of the situation and drove away from the parking lot, her anxiety mounting as she watched her daughter continue her conversation with Shantel through the rear-view mirror. With each passing second, her fear of Alicia intensified, and she longed to reach the safety of their home. She knew she had to share the events of the afternoon with Damian.

As soon as they arrived, Alicia wasted no time, leaping out of the car and racing into the house. Sarah breathed a sigh of relief upon spotting Damian's car in the driveway. She followed Alicia inside, determined to intercept her before she retreated to the solitude of her room for the remainder of the night.

"Alicia, you need to inform your father about your attitude when I picked you up," Sarah insisted, but Alicia seemed oblivious, fully engrossed in a deep conversation with Shantel. "Alicia, I'm speaking to you."

Alicia groaned and spun around, fixing her mother with a scathing glare. "CAN'T YOU SEE I'M TALKING TO MY FRIEND? HOW ABOUT YOU WAIT UNTIL I'M DONE?" she screamed at the top of her lungs.

"Now, hold on a second. You do not speak to

your mother in that tone," Damian interjected, his voice brimming with stern authority.

"Of course, you would take her side," Alicia rolled her eyes dismissively. "Let me guess, you're just like everyone else who believes Shantel isn't real. Well, guess what? I couldn't care less about your opinion. Believe whatever you want. I know Shantel is real, and she's my friend. My only friend. I'd appreciate it if the two of you would stay out of my business and refrain from interrupting me when I'm trying to have a conversation with my friend. I'll be up in my room. Do not follow me. My conversations with Shantel are meant to stay private!" With that, Alicia sprinted up the stairs, slamming her bedroom door with such force that the walls trembled.

Sarah let out a heavy sigh, relief mingled with frustration evident in her voice. "And now you know how my day went after picking her up," she confided to Damian. "I don't know what to do with her anymore. You should have seen the attitude she gave me when I asked her not to talk to Shantel in public. It's getting worse."

Damian understood the gravity of the situation, his brows knitted in concern. They were well aware that Alicia had been struggling with behavioral issues, but her behavior today was the most severe they had witnessed since they moved to the neighborhood. Together, they realized they had to uncover the root cause of their daughter's distress before it irreparably consumed her.

∞ ∞ ∞

Chapter 10

Sarah's heart had always yearned for a loving family with Damian, but the reality of adopting Alicia had taken an unexpected turn. Despite their hopes that this difficult phase would pass, each passing day revealed Alicia's condition deteriorating further. The once ethereal friendship between Alicia and Shantel now seemed to transcend mere imagination, leaving Sarah and Damian deeply concerned about their daughter's grip on reality.

On a serene Saturday afternoon, Alicia found herself outside, immersed in the playground Damian had painstakingly constructed in the hopes of bringing solace to their troubled daughter. Sarah stood in the warmth of the kitchen, peering through the window with a mix of surprise and anticipation. Alicia, who had previously shown no interest in the swings, now sat upon one, gently propelling herself back and forth.

"What's going on?" Damian's voice broke the

hushed atmosphere as he approached Sarah from behind.

"You've got to see this. Alicia is actually on the swings," Sarah whispered, her voice filled with a mixture of astonishment and hope.

In a state of disbelief, Damian joined her at the window, his eyes widening as they beheld the unexpected sight. Just a month prior, Damian had completed the playground, but Alicia had shown no inclination to explore its offerings. In fact, she hadn't even acknowledged Damian's efforts when he eagerly presented it to her. Instead, she had bypassed the playground, retreating to a solitary corner of the yard. Yet, on this remarkable day, Alicia had chosen to embrace the swings, and her parents couldn't contain their joy.

"I don't believe it," Damian murmured, his voice laced with wonder. "What do you think changed in her?"

"I have no idea," Sarah replied, her voice tinged with a mixture of bewilderment and cautious optimism. "All she said was that she was going outside and left. You know how she is, never wanting to say more than a few words to us," she added, releasing a nervous laugh.

"Sarah, do you think this might signify the end of whatever she was going through?" Damian's voice brimmed with a mixture of hope and vulnerability.

"I truly hope so," Sarah replied, her voice filled with a blend of longing and trepidation. She began making her way towards the front door, her resolve firm.

"Where are you going?" Damian inquired, his concern evident.

"I want to see what's happening. Is that wrong? Should I refrain from intervening?" Sarah's mind swirled with worry, fearing that any action she took might inadvertently push Alicia further away.

"I don't think it would be a problem," Damian reassured her, his voice gentle. "Moreover, considering the tragic incident that occurred near our home, it's only natural for a concerned parent to keep a watchful eye over our daughter."

"Good point," Sarah replied, a sense of relief coloring her words. With newfound reassurance, she stepped outside, her gaze falling upon Alicia, who was joyfully engrossed in the rhythmic motion of the swing. This was the moment Sarah had yearned for since the challenges with Alicia had surfaced—a glimpse of her daughter, once more embodying the spirited girl they had welcomed into their lives.

Sarah treaded cautiously, aware that she mustn't startle Alicia, still respecting her daughter's need for privacy. There were occasions when Alicia would display a prickly attitude whenever Sarah broached the subject of Shantel. Sarah couldn't discern anything unusual about Alicia's current actions, but she resolved to be vigilant and handle her daughter with care.

Returning to the front door, Sarah found Damian waiting outside, his face etched with curiosity. "What's going on?" he inquired.

"Based on what I observed, nothing significant for now. Alicia was swinging, but I couldn't determine if she was conversing with Shantel or not. I didn't want to startle her or provoke her anger. I thought I might pretend to tend to some gardening tasks and listen discreetly," Sarah explained, her voice filled with concern.

"Good idea. We don't want her to feel like we're prying," Damian agreed. "I was so elated to see her using the playground that I didn't consider..." His voice trailed off as his gaze fixed upon the yard.

"What is it? What's happening?" Sarah felt a surge of apprehension, reluctant to turn around and confront what might await her.

"I'm not sure what's transpiring, but Alicia abruptly ceased swinging and is now sitting motionless on the swing," Damian revealed. "It was peculiar. She just stopped abruptly, as if influenced by an unseen force."

With trepidation, Sarah slowly pivoted, her eyes locking onto the scene her husband had described. Alicia sat on the swing, immobile, engrossed in a conversation with someone Sarah couldn't perceive.

"I need to investigate," Sarah whispered, tiptoeing stealthily behind her daughter. It wasn't until she drew nearer that she discerned Alicia's hushed words. Sarah inwardly sighed, her fears confirmed—Alicia was still accompanied by Shantel. She inched closer, desperate to eavesdrop on her daughter's dialogue with this unseen friend.

"Don't worry, Shantel. We will rectify this. With your assistance, we'll locate him," Alicia asserted, her voice resolute. "We can't give up."

What were they striving to accomplish? Whom were they seeking? Sarah's mind spun with a torrent of inquiries. Alicia's conversation with Shantel carried an air of determination, signaling her unwavering commitment to find a man. This revelation filled Sarah with unease.

"I understand it's been a while, but we must ascertain if he's still out there," Alicia continued, her discourse with Shantel intensifying. "Do you want him to harm another girl like he did to you?

No. I thought not. That's precisely why we must bring him to justice."

Sarah's heart sank as her daughter's words hung in the air. The gravity of the situation weighed heavily upon her. Alicia, driven by a resolute purpose, was on a quest to confront a man who had caused Shantel harm. The thought of Alicia embarking on such a perilous endeavor filled Sarah with anxiety and a deep sense of maternal protectiveness.

The weight of Sarah's pounding heart reverberated through her chest as she absorbed the words that reached her ears. Her thoughts were clouded by fear, worried that her daughter's mind had been tainted by this imaginary companion, leading her down a path of harm. Each passing day seemed to escalate the situation as Alicia continued to believe in Shantel's existence.

Wanting to uncover the truth from Alicia, Sarah understood the delicate nature of approaching her daughter. Any misstep could trigger explosive outbursts, and being outside only heightened the risk of neighbors overhearing. With caution as her guide, she inched closer to Alicia.

"Alicia?"

"Shantel, we've got this," Alicia dismissed

her mother, her attention solely focused on her unseen confidante. "Just provide me with any information I need, and I'll track down this man. I'll make sure he pays for what he did to you."

"Alicia?" Sarah raised her voice, growing more insistent.

Rolling her eyes, Alicia turned her attention away from Shantel. "I'll get rid of her so we can continue our conversation," she assured her invisible companion before finally acknowledging her mother. "What do you want? I told you I wanted to be alone out here."

"I know, but you've been out here for hours. I wanted to check in and see how everything was going," Sarah maintained a composed demeanor.

"I'm busy. I'll come back inside when I'm ready. Is that okay with you?"

"Yes, that's perfectly fine," Sarah nodded, masking her concern with a reassuring smile. "So, I overheard you talking to Shantel."

"WHAT? HOW DO YOU KNOW?" Alicia erupted, her voice laced with anger. "ARE YOU LISTENING TO MY CONVERSATIONS NOW?"

"Please, calm down. I didn't mean to eavesdrop on your conversation. I was coming out here to work in the garden when I heard you talking," Sarah pleaded, attempting to defuse the mounting tension.

"Fine. So, you overheard me talking to Shantel," Alicia dismissed the significance, feigning nonchalance. "Is there anything else you want?" Her shoulders shrugged, irritation evident.

"Well, I was wondering what exactly you were discussing with her," Sarah pressed gently.

"Nothing, Mom. Just typical stuff girls our age talk about." Alicia evaded specifics, hoping her evasiveness would prompt her mother to leave her alone.

"Are you sure about that? From what I heard, it didn't sound like an ordinary conversation. Which man were you referring to when you said you'd find him and make him pay for what he did?"

Alicia's eyes widened as the realization sunk in, exposing just how much of her conversation with Shantel her mother had overheard. "How much more did you hear?" Alicia retorted with a sneer.

"Nothing," Sarah replied, her response calculated to avoid escalating the tension.

Alicia's anger flared, her disbelief evident as she confronted her mother. "No. I don't believe you. You heard more than you should. Why? Just why would you stand there and listen to what I'm saying with my friend?" Her frustration grew palpable.

"Alicia, you keep so much hidden from your father and me. We have to do whatever we can to find out what is going on in your life."

"Even if it means invading my privacy?" Alicia crossed her arms, her eyes fixed on her mother. "I don't believe you." She abruptly got off the swing, her determination clear.

Sarah's heart sank as Alicia prepared to leave. She desperately hoped they were making progress in uncovering the truth about their daughter. If Alicia ran off now, it would mean they weren't getting any closer to understanding what was wrong.

"Why must you know everything I'm doing? I came out here for privacy since you and Dad are always outside my bedroom door listening to my conversations with Shantel! Now, you're following me outside. The one place I thought I had some privacy! Just leave me alone!" Alicia's voice carried the weight of frustration as she stormed past Damian, pushing her way into the house on her way to her room.

Feeling defeated, Sarah retreated inside, her spirit deflated. She spotted Damian wearing a shocked expression. "Where did she go?"

"To her room. What happened? I've never seen her that angry before," Damian replied, concern etched on his face.

"It was horrible, Damian. I overheard her talking to Shantel about finding some guy. She was saying something about how she'll find that man and make him pay. It was terrifying. It's as if she was talking about killing someone. When I asked her what she meant, she exploded, accusing us of never giving her any privacy. How can we when she acts this way?"

Damian enveloped Sarah in a comforting embrace, attempting to soothe her troubled mind. "I don't know what to make of any of this. But we'll have to speak to her teacher about it, let him know what happened. I'm not sure what else we can do at this point."

"You know I'm not one to give up, but she's pushing me to my limits," Sarah sobbed. "And what about the counselor at school? I thought he was supposed to help us. It doesn't seem like he's making any difference."

"Tell you what. Tomorrow morning, I'll call the school and inform them about what happened today. I'll let them know that things haven't improved at home. You've been the one making all the calls since this started, so let me handle it now. Give yourself a break. You need it. We'll see what Mr. Bailey and Mr. Sanders have to say, and then we'll take it from there."

"Good idea. I don't know how much more of this I can bear. Damian, she's making me question my own sanity. She tried to downplay what I heard as if it meant nothing. But those words... they sounded like they came from someone capable of committing murder. I just want our daughter back."

"We will get her back," Damian reassured his wife, his voice filled with determination. "It'll take time, but I know we'll bring back the Alicia we know, our loving daughter. First, we need to get her the help she needs."

Sarah's racing thoughts began to settle as she found solace in Damian's support. Tomorrow morning, he would make the calls to the school, hoping to find answers from the counselor. She knew it would be challenging to erase the haunting words she had overheard Alicia uttering in the yard, but she had to approach everything one step at a time.

∞ ∞ ∞

Chapter 11

The atmosphere in the neighborhood had grown tense ever since Alicia's explosive outburst in their front yard that Sunday morning. The incident had caused a ripple effect, leading people to avoid the Atkinson family. Nonetheless, Damian kept his promise and promptly called the school the following morning. The teacher and counselor assured him that they would keep an eye on Alicia and inform the couple if anything concerning arose. Two weeks had passed since then, and finally, it seemed like things were looking up. Sarah and Damian hadn't received any distressing calls from the school, and they believed their daughter was gradually moving on from her troubled friendship with Shantel.

However, on that fateful Monday afternoon, Sarah received an unexpected call that shattered their sense of relief. Answering the phone with trepidation, she spoke, her voice betraying her unease. "Hello?"

"Mrs. Atkinson? This is Mr. Avila," the

principal's voice resonated on the other end.

"Mr. Avila. Hi," Sarah replied, immediately sensing that a call from the principal at noon couldn't possibly bring good news. "Did something happen with Alicia?"

"I don't feel comfortable discussing this over the phone. Could you and your husband please come and pick your daughter up? We'll discuss the situation when you arrive," Mr. Avila requested, his tone grave.

Sarah's voice quivered as she replied, "Yes, of course. Let me call my husband now, and we'll be right over." She ended the call and quickly dialed Damian's number, her anxiety palpable.

"Sarah, what's wrong?" Damian answered, noting the urgency in his wife's voice. It was evident that something was amiss for her to be calling him during work hours.

"Damian, we have to get down to Alicia's school now. Her principal called and told us to come pick her up."

Damian swiftly shut down his computer and grabbed his coat, his mind racing with worry. "Did he tell you why?"

"No, but I'm sure it has to be serious. He said he didn't feel comfortable talking to me about it on the phone. Damian, I'm scared," Sarah confided, her fear seeping through her words.

"I'm heading out of the office right now. Wait for me, and I'll come and get you so we can go to the school together. And Sarah? I know it's hard, but try to stay calm until we know for sure what happened," Damian reassured her, his voice filled with concern.

Damian arrived home shortly after their phone call. Sarah was already waiting outside, her anxiety visible as she rushed to the car upon his arrival. Her leg trembled throughout the drive to the school, despite Damian's attempts to soothe her. Pulling into the parking lot, they walked together into the school building. As they entered, they spotted Mr. Avila standing in the lobby, accompanied by Alicia.

"Mr. and Mrs. Atkinson, thank you for coming in. Please, follow me to my office," the principal greeted them, his voice tinged with seriousness. They trailed behind him, entering his office while Alicia sullenly took a seat, crossing her arms in annoyance. Mr. Avila addressed her, his tone firm. "Alicia, would you like to tell your parents what happened this afternoon?"

"No," she snapped, her defiance evident.

Mr. Avila glanced at Sarah and Damian, retrieving a knife from his desk drawer. "Does this knife look familiar?"

Confusion washed over Damian and Sarah as they exchanged bewildered glances. They had never seen this knife before, and it certainly did not belong to them. Moreover, it was not a type of knife they owned or kept in their house.

"Sorry, but I don't know who that belongs to," Damian responded, his voice tinged with bewilderment.

"That's very interesting because Alicia was caught with this knife today. A student asked her how she was, and she pulled the knife on them. Luckily, a teacher happened to be passing by and intervened, stopping the altercation. When confronted, Alicia turned the knife toward the teacher, but they managed to disarm her. That's when they brought her into my office. I assumed the knife came from home. It looks like the type one would bring when hunting," Mr. Avila explained, his words heavy with concern.

"I've never been hunting in my life. I wouldn't know anything about hunting tools," Damian stated, his confusion deepening.

"And we don't keep any weapons in the house," Sarah added, her voice tinged with worry.

"I've been trying to get it out of Alicia where the knife came from, but she won't give me an answer. All she keeps saying is that it isn't my business," Mr. Avila shared, frustration evident in his tone. He looked at Alicia and requested, "Would you mind going outside and sitting in the lobby while I talk to your parents?"

"I don't care," Alicia shrugged her shoulders, her face displaying a mix of indifference and resentment. "I'm used to people talking about me behind my back," she said dismissively as she exited the office, leaving her bewildered parents and the concerned principal behind.

Mr. Avila's office was a small, dimly lit space adorned with framed awards and diplomas that lined the walls. The desk, cluttered with papers and a computer, served as the focal point of the room. As Sarah and Damian took their seats, anxiety filled the air, thickening with each passing moment.

Mr. Avila leaned forward in his chair, his eyes fixed on the couple. Worry etched across his face, he began to address the gravity of Alicia's actions. His voice carried a mix of concern and frustration, emphasizing the impact her behavior had on the school. He spoke of her frequent disruptions in class, her growing list of disciplinary issues, and the resulting strain it placed on teachers and staff.

"You see, this isn't the first time Alicia has caused trouble in the classroom. We've tried various interventions, but her behavior is becoming increasingly problematic," Mr. Avila explained, his voice tinged with exasperation. "But today, it went to a whole new level. Bringing a weapon into the school is a grave offense, and we cannot overlook it. The safety of our students and staff is paramount."

Damian interjected, his voice filled with genuine concern. "We genuinely have no idea where she could have obtained that weapon. We don't own anything like it, and Alicia doesn't have any friends who might have given it to her."

As Mr. Avila listened, he scribbled notes, his expression growing more serious. "This is deeply troubling. Alicia's actions endangered many people within these walls. As per our school's policy, she will be suspended for one week. It could have been worse; expulsion is the usual consequence for bringing a weapon to school. I implore you, during this suspension, seek the help she needs. We cannot allow this behavior to continue."

"Thank you for your understanding, Mr. Avila," Damian replied, his voice laced with gratitude. "We will do everything within our power to find the appropriate support for Alicia."

Leaving Mr. Avila's office, Sarah and Damian walked into the lobby where Alicia sat with an air of defiance. Sarah's voice softened as she addressed her daughter, "Sweetie, let's go."

Alicia's response was laced with hostility. "Where are we going?"

Damian's voice grew stern. "Watch your tone. We're going home to discuss what happened today. Your actions have resulted in a one-week suspension from school."

Alicia hid her satisfaction behind a forced neutral expression. She couldn't let her parents see how pleased she was with the suspension. It provided her with a week of solitude to focus on helping Shantel without any interference.

The drive back home was filled with an oppressive silence, Sarah and Damian deep in thought, strategizing their approach. They acknowledged their own responsibility in allowing Alicia's communication with Shantel to escalate, but they were determined to put an end to this dangerous behavior. No longer would Alicia's hurtful words and defiant attitude be the primary concern. She had crossed a line by bringing a weapon to school, and they couldn't ignore the potential harm it posed to others.

Once inside the house, Damian called for Alicia to sit down, his tone firm. She rolled her eyes, displaying her annoyance. Didn't they understand that she had important work to do and wanted to be left alone?

"After what happened today, you have the

audacity to give us attitude," Damian reproached, his frustration palpable. He knew he should have chosen his words more carefully, but Alicia's behavior was testing his patience. "I had to leave my job and sacrifice a day's pay because of the stunt you pulled. Do you grasp the consequences of your actions? Where did you get that weapon?"

Alicia turned away from her father, her eyes avoiding his probing gaze. The weight of his question hung in the air, unanswered. Sensing an opportunity to bridge the gap, Sarah softly whispered to Damian, her voice filled with determination. She had always been the one to keep her composure when dealing with Alicia's outbursts.

"Let me give it a try," Sarah murmured. Moving to sit beside Alicia on the couch, she gently placed a hand on her daughter's shoulder. "Sweetie, we're genuinely concerned for your safety and the well-being of everyone at your school. We just want to understand where you obtained the weapon. We won't be angry if you tell us the truth."

"I don't want to talk about it," Alicia replied, her voice barely above a whisper, her gaze fixed on the ground.

Sarah persisted, her voice filled with empathy. "Is it because you're afraid of getting the person who gave it to you in trouble? Please, don't worry about that right now. This is about you. Mr. Avila suspended you for a week because you brought a weapon to school. Do you realize the implications it will have on your permanent record? We're not trying to invade your privacy, Alicia. We're only asking for the truth because we care about you."

"I can't tell you the truth," Alicia's frustration seeped into her voice.

Damian joined in, sitting on the other side of Alicia. "Why not? Who are you trying to protect?"

"No one!" Alicia's voice cracked, her frustration turning into desperation. "I can't tell you the truth because I genuinely don't know who the knife belongs to!"

Confusion and concern clouded Sarah's face. "What do you mean you don't know who it belongs to? How did it end up in your possession?"

"That's what I'm trying to explain!" Alicia's tears began to flow. "I don't know how I got it. When I opened my backpack at school, it was there. I took it out and hid it in my pocket because I didn't want anyone to find it while my backpack was in the closet. And then, during recess, when students and teachers started bothering me, I took it out. I never intended to hurt anyone. It was more of a warning, a way to make them leave me alone." Alicia's sobs grew louder. "Maybe if people actually listened to me instead of labeling me as a bad person, I would feel more comfortable telling the truth." With that, Alicia stormed off to her room, escaping her parents' bewildered stares.

Sarah turned to Damian, her expression a mix of worry and confusion. "What do we do now?"

Damian sighed, his voice tinged with concern. "Something isn't right. What we just witnessed was not the same girl we saw in the principal's office. It's almost as if there's a split personality at play."

Sarah nodded in agreement. "I had the same thought. She needs more help than we initially believed. Speaking to counselors might not be enough. You know what I think might be beneficial? Getting her tested. Perhaps there's an underlying condition that went unnoticed for so long. She's been passed around in foster homes, and her health was likely neglected."

"Well, we have a week to make sure we get everything sorted out. With any luck, we might finally uncover what's truly going on with her," Damian remarked.

"I'll call her doctor right away, explaining the urgency of the situation," Sarah said, her fingers trembling slightly as she reached for her phone.

"And I'll inform my boss about the family emergency and request the week off," Damian added, determination evident in his voice.

Sarah anxiously awaited the doctor's response, grateful that Damian was finally stepping up and actively participating in Alicia's journey. She hoped that they were finally on the right path toward understanding their daughter's struggles and finding the help she needed so desperately.

∞ ∞ ∞

Chapter 12

Sarah and Damian felt a glimmer of hope as they embarked on their journey to uncover the truth about Alicia. They had scheduled an appointment with Dr. Dixon, Alicia's doctor, later in the week, desperately seeking her expertise to shed light on their daughter's mysterious condition.

Nervously, the trio sat in the waiting room of Dr. Dixon's office, Alicia's irritation palpable as she brooded over her parents' constant presence. Her suspension from school had granted her an unexpected respite, a chance to plot her vengeance against Shantel's murderer, but her parents had been relentless in their vigilance ever since that fateful day when Alicia was discovered with the knife.

"Sweetie, please try to understand. Dr. Dixon is here to help us figure things out," Sarah reassured her daughter, her voice filled with genuine concern.

"I'm fine, there's nothing wrong with me," muttered Alicia sullenly. "I don't know why you dragged me to this place."

A sigh escaped Sarah's lips, and she turned to Damian, seeking validation. "We're doing the right thing, aren't we?"

"Absolutely. We have no other choice. Alicia needs help," Damian affirmed, his voice laced with determination. He glanced at his daughter, her defiant demeanor not deterring him. "You saw how quickly her mood shifted when we asked about the knife. There's something beneath the surface, something we need to uncover. She may not want to be here, but it's what's best for her."

Sarah nodded, her worry etched on her face. "I know you're right. I just hate that she's angry with us."

"Sarah, she would be angry regardless. We have to stand firm and face this once and for all," Damian reassured her, his hand gently caressing her leg. "Remember what Mr. Avila said. We're fortunate he didn't expel her for bringing a weapon to school. The life she had before we adopted her influenced his decision to give her a suspension. Discovering the truth will set us on the right path."

Their conversation was interrupted as Dr. Dixon emerged from her office. "Alicia?"

Rising from their seats, Sarah and Damian followed Alicia into the doctor's office. Astonishment clouded Alicia's face as she turned to her parents. "Wait, you're coming in with me? Are you kidding me?"

"We need to understand what's happening and talk to your doctor," Damian explained as Dr. Dixon ushered them into her main office.

"Please, have a seat here, Mr. and Mrs. Atkinson," Dr. Dixon gestured, her tone warm and welcoming. Meanwhile, Alicia was guided down the hall by a nurse to the exam room. Dr. Dixon took a moment to retrieve her notes on Alicia from her desk. "Let's discuss the reason for your visit. Alicia was suspended from school for bringing a weapon, and when confronted, she claimed ignorance about its origin. Additionally, Mr. Atkinson, you mentioned that Alicia has been conversing with an imaginary friend whom she believes is real?"

"Yes, that's correct," Damian confirmed. "My wife overheard Alicia engaged in deep conversations with this friend named Shantel. Alicia behaves as though this person is physically present." He turned to Sarah. "What did you hear her say the other day that frightened you?"

Sarah recounted the incident with a tinge of trepidation. "Yes, Doctor. She was outside in our front yard, and I overheard her vowing to find the person responsible for Shantel's fate. When I inquired about whom she was referring to and what had happened to Shantel, she threw a tantrum and fled to her room."

Taking diligent notes, Dr. Dixon absorbed the information. "This is indeed intriguing, and it appears that something is amiss. Given the limited medical history available due to the lack of record-keeping by the foster homes Alicia resided in prior to your adoption, I believe it's time to conduct a comprehensive physical examination, including tests to assess her brain function. I can perform the necessary tests here and have the results within a few hours."

"Doctor, we would greatly appreciate any efforts you can make to help us understand and assist her," Sarah expressed her gratitude.

Dr. Dixon nodded reassuringly. "It's my pleasure, Mrs. Atkinson. You and your husband need not remain here throughout the entire process. I will have everything prepared, tests completed, and results ready in three hours. Return then, and we will discuss my findings in detail."

****

Anxiety gnawed at Sarah and Damian's nerves as they remained close to the doctor's office, their minds consumed by worry over Alicia's impending test results. The passing of three hours felt like an interminable stretch of time, each minute laden with anticipation. Damian offered a comforting gesture, clasping his wife's hand firmly as they made their way back to the office. Leaning in, he whispered words of reassurance in Sarah's ear, emphasizing the importance of getting Alicia the help she needed.

"Absolutely. Our priority is Alicia's well-being," Sarah affirmed, her voice laced with determination.

Returning to Dr. Dixon's office, their eyes met with hers, brimming with anticipation and concern. Sarah's heart raced, anxiety gripping her as she awaited the verdict. "Doctor, what did you find? What's wrong with Alicia?" Her voice quivered with a mix of fear and hope.

Dr. Dixon met their gaze, a perplexed expression on her face. "That's the puzzling part. Despite conducting three different brain tests, we haven't identified any abnormalities or issues."

"How can that be?" Damian's voice rose, his frustration evident. He rose from his seat, a surge of emotions welling up within him. "You heard everything we shared. How can you dismiss her behavior as normal? Talking to an imaginary friend, bringing weapons to school, and making threats against other students."

Dr. Dixon maintained her composure, her tone steady. "I understand there's something unusual about her behavior, but it doesn't appear to stem from a physical ailment. This goes beyond my field of expertise, but I believe Alicia's challenges lie in the realm of mental health. I strongly advise seeking the assistance of a psychologist."

Damian's frustration was palpable. "We've already pursued that avenue. The psychologist couldn't pinpoint any issues either. You were our last hope." He turned to Sarah, a sense of resignation shadowing his features. "Let's go and bring Alicia home. It's evident that we won't find any answers here."

Disappointment mingled with a sense of helplessness as Sarah and Damian prepared to collect Alicia and depart from the doctor's office, their search for answers once again leading them down an uncertain path.

****

The car ride home was cloaked in an eerie silence, heavy with unspoken tension. Alicia brooded in the backseat, her anger at her parents palpable. Since leaving the doctor's office, she hadn't uttered a single word to them, her resentment simmering beneath the surface. All she yearned for was the solace of home, a sanctuary where she could escape the distressing events of the day. Meanwhile, Damian seethed with fury, directing his anger towards Dr. Dixon for failing to uncover any issues plaguing their daughter, leaving them back at square one. Sarah, on the other hand, found herself caught in a whirlwind of emotions. She despised the fact that the doctor couldn't identify any problems with Alicia, yet she was repulsed by Damian's behavior at the office. Dr. Dixon was merely trying to assist, and it wasn't her fault that the tests yielded no results. Although Sarah felt upset, she refrained from venting her frustration towards the doctor.

As Damian pulled into the driveway, Alicia swiftly exited the car, her impatience evident as she tapped her foot against the ground, awaiting her father's unlocking of the front door. The moment he obliged, she wasted no time darting inside and up the stairs, determined to seclude herself in her room.

"Alicia, we need to talk..." Damian's voice carried up the staircase, but before he could finish his sentence, Alicia abruptly shut her bedroom door, shutting herself off from the impending confrontation.

"Let her be," Sarah interjected, her voice tinged with weariness as she ascended the stairs towards the bedroom she shared with Damian.

"What do you mean?" Damian retorted,

following closely behind. "There's clearly something seriously wrong with her, and we need to address it head-on."

"You know, you really are something else," Sarah paused in front of Alicia's closed door, turning to face her husband, her expression a mixture of disbelief and disappointment. "You're hardly ever home. You don't witness what I witness when I'm here with Alicia. Maybe that's the crux of the issue. She's endured bouncing between foster homes, and just when she thought she had finally found a family, she realized her father is never around."

"Me? You're placing the blame on me? What about you? You continually make excuses for her behavior. This is all your fault," Damian retorted, his voice laced with accusation. "I didn't see you getting upset with the doctor today. And let's not forget who made all those calls to the school. It was me. I'm the one doing the dirty work while you sit back and coddle her. No wonder neither the doctor nor the counselors have found anything wrong with her!"

Unknown to her parents, Alicia had crept closer to her bedroom door, which she cracked open to eavesdrop on their conversation. Her heart sank as their words collided, laying blame upon each other for her troubled behavior.

"I tried to tell them, Shantel. I really did,"

Alicia whispered to the imaginary presence beside her. "But they ignored me. They ignored us. And today, they took me to the doctor for no reason. Dad was furious that the doctor couldn't find anything wrong with my brain. Why would they find something? You're here with me, talking to me. I can hear you."

Retreating to her bed, Alicia curled up, bringing her knees close to her chin, as the conversation between her parents continued to echo through the door. "I won't blame myself for their arguments. I didn't ask them to fight. They should have listened to me from the beginning."

The room descended into silence, the argument between her parents abruptly halting, and Alicia heard the sound of their footsteps fading in opposite directions throughout the house. Quietly, she approached her bedroom door and cautiously opened it, revealing an empty corridor. "Good. They're gone," she muttered to herself. "Now, let's resume our discussion about the plan. Shantel, you have to tell me who this man is so I know who to seek out. Leave the rest to me. I'll know what to do when I find him."

There was much to be done, but Alicia's determination to locate the man responsible for Shantel's death burned within her. The police had allowed him to evade justice once before, but Alicia refused to let history repeat itself.

"Don't worry about their argument, Shantel. It's over now. I don't care how my behavior affects my parents. They aren't my real parents, just like your parents weren't. I'm on a mission for you, and that's the only thing that matters to me. Sometimes, achieving a mission comes at a high price. If helping you strains the bond between my parents, so be it. As long as, in the end, your murderer is apprehended, it will all be worth it."

A chilling smile crept across Alicia's face as she contemplated her resolve. "Soon, your killer will be caught, and I will be the instrument of his downfall."

∞ ∞ ∞

Chapter 13

Sarah's heart sank as she grappled with the unsettling turn her life had taken that day, following the visit to Alicia's doctor. She had secretly hoped that Dr. Dixon would uncover some underlying issue, providing an explanation for the recent troubles. But her hopes were dashed when the results came back, revealing nothing out of the ordinary. The disappointment weighed heavily on her, exacerbating the tension that had been building within her.

The fight with Damian had taken an unexpectedly dark turn, unlike anything they had experienced in their years of marriage. As she sat upright in bed, a profound sense of unease enveloped her, contrasting with Damian's peaceful slumber. How could he remain unaffected by the turmoil that consumed her?

Sleep eluded her, and she grew restless and bored. She cast a glance at Damian, briefly considering waking him up for a conversation. But she hesitated, knowing that he would likely resent being disturbed due to her inability to find solace in sleep.

Frustration gnawed at her as she continued to toss and turn, finding no respite. Determined to alleviate her restlessness, she resolved to venture downstairs to the kitchen, recalling how this had once worked during her youthful days when sleep eluded her. A late-night snack seemed like a fitting distraction.

As she descended the stairs, her gaze fell upon Alicia's closed bedroom door, and a sigh escaped her lips. She longed for her daughter to be more open, less secretive. Temptation briefly flickered within her, urging her to barge into Alicia's room. However, she quickly dismissed the idea, cognizant of the strained relationship between them and the potential repercussions it could entail. Alicia was already resentful for being taken to see Dr. Dixon, and intruding upon her sanctuary now would only exacerbate her mood.

Reaching the kitchen, Sarah flicked on the light switch, illuminating the room with a soft glow. But her tranquility was abruptly shattered when she let out a piercing scream upon spotting Alicia by the sink, clutching a knife tightly in her hand. "Alicia? Alicia?" she called out, her voice trembling, hesitant to approach any closer. Alicia stood motionless, her gaze fixed and distant.

"Alicia?" Sarah's voice quivered, taking a few tentative steps forward, yet eliciting no response from her daughter.

Sarah fought to maintain her composure, her mind racing as she contemplated the best course of action. She yearned for answers, for an explanation of Alicia's inexplicable behavior. "Damian?" she called out, her voice carrying a hint of desperation, though it barely reached the upstairs. "Damian?" she repeated, her voice growing louder.

Turning her attention back to Alicia, she noted the girl's unyielding stillness. "Alicia, I'm not angry. Just put the knife down, and we can talk about this," she pleaded in a last-ditch effort to reason with her daughter. Yet Alicia remained frozen, seemingly unaffected by her mother's entreaties.

Realizing that her options were dwindling, Sarah resolved to seek Damian's help. She sprinted back upstairs, rushing into their bedroom, and feverishly shook Damian awake. "Wake up! Damian! Wake up!" she implored urgently.

Rubbing the sleep from his eyes, Damian yawned, his voice filled with weariness. "What is it now, Sarah? It's three in the morning."

"I don't care what time it is. You need to come downstairs. Alicia is in the kitchen, holding a knife."

"Are you certain you weren't dreaming? Given what she was caught doing at school, I can understand why you might imagine something like this."

"Damian, I know what I saw. She was standing there, holding the knife in her hands. Initially, she was lurking in the darkness. I turned on the lights, and that's when I saw her. I tried to get her to explain, but she remained unresponsive."

She didn't need to say more for Damian to realize the gravity of the situation. Rising from the bed, he accompanied her to the kitchen, Sarah gripping his arm tightly. He halted at the entrance, a mix of concern and confusion etched across his face as he beheld Alicia standing in the same spot where Sarah had left her.

"Alicia? It's your father. Why don't you put the knife down and come over here? Let's talk about what's going on," Damian implored gently, his voice tinged with apprehension. Alicia remained immobile, prompting Damian to exchange a worried glance with Sarah. "Is she behaving the same way as when you found her?" he inquired.

"Yes," Sarah nodded, her voice laden with anxiety. "I can't seem to reach her. Damian, what should we do? Should we call 911?"

"Not at this moment. Let me try," Damian remarked, mustering his resolve. He approached Alicia cautiously, placing a gentle hand on her shoulder. "Alicia, sweetheart, please put the knife down. We're here for you. We want to understand. Can you talk to us?"

Alicia's vacant stare remained fixed, her grip on the knife unyielding. Damian's concern deepened, realizing that their attempts to communicate were falling on deaf ears. He made a split-second decision, reaching for his phone to dial emergency services.

As the operator answered, Damian quickly explained the situation, emphasizing the urgency and the potential danger involved. The operator assured him that help was on the way and advised them to stay on the line until the authorities arrived.

Minutes felt like an eternity as they waited anxiously for the sound of sirens. Sarah clung to Damian, seeking solace and strength in his presence. Alicia remained motionless, a silent enigma in their midst.

Finally, the wailing sirens pierced the night, their sound growing louder until they reached a crescendo outside their home. Law enforcement and medical professionals flooded into the kitchen, their training taking over as they assessed the situation and approached Alicia with caution. They successfully disarmed her, ensuring the safety of everyone involved.

As Alicia was taken into custody for an evaluation, Sarah and Damian watched with heavy hearts. Mixed emotions swirled within them—fear, confusion, and an overwhelming desire to understand what had led their daughter to this point.

In the days that followed, Alicia received professional help and support. The incident marked the beginning of a long and challenging journey for their family—a journey that would involve therapy, counseling, and the search for answers.

Sarah and Damian remained steadfast in their commitment to Alicia's well-being, doing everything in their power to help her heal and rebuild her life. They sought solace in each other, drawing strength from their love and determination to navigate the difficult road ahead.

While the path remained uncertain, they clung to the hope that with time, understanding, and unwavering support, Alicia would find her way back to them, and together, they would rebuild their shattered lives.

****

The next morning, the tension in the air was palpable as the family gathered around the breakfast table. Rays of sunlight filtered through the windows, casting a warm glow on their troubled faces. The clinking of plates and utensils provided a stark contrast to the brewing storm of emotions.

Damian, his brow furrowed, broke the uneasy silence. "She's lying!" His voice carried an undercurrent of frustration and concern, his words cutting through the stillness of the room.

Sarah, seated across from Damian, raised an eyebrow, her voice laced with a mix of doubt and empathy. "What do you mean she's lying? She told us she had a nightmare." Sarah, ever the optimist, sought to give Alicia the benefit of the doubt, hoping that her daughter was telling the truth.

Damian, pouring his coffee with a hint of agitation, set the cup down with a thud. "And you believed that story? You saw what I saw, Sarah. That wasn't a girl having a nightmare. There was something more going on in her mind. Something sinister." His words hung in the air, heavy with an unspoken truth. His conviction in the need for professional help was resolute.

Meanwhile, Alicia, eavesdropping on the argument from the staircase, froze in her tracks, her heart pounding. Anger surged within her, a fiery defiance ignited by her father's insinuations. "What gives him the right to say that about me?" she thought, her face contorted into a scowl. "I'm not the dangerous one here. The murderer out there is the dangerous one. They need to stop messing with my plan to catch this man."

Sarah, her voice tinged with disbelief, interjected, challenging Damian's assertions. "Dangerous? You think she's dangerous now? This is our daughter you're talking about." The weight of the situation bore down on her, and she struggled to comprehend the conflicting perspectives. "Yesterday, you wanted her to get mental health help. And now you're telling me she's dangerous. Which is it?"

Exasperation seeped into Damian's voice as he shouted, his frustration boiling over. "BOTH! And this is why she needs to get help. I wish you would open your eyes and see that!"

Sarah's arms flew up in exasperation, her voice filled with a mix of anguish and frustration. "Oh, so now it's my fault? That's what it comes down to, isn't it?" Her eyes searched Damian's face for a glimmer of understanding. "You're blaming me because I'm the one home with her and never picked up on any of this. Yet, you're home whenever you're not working at the dealership and think you know everything about Alicia."

Damian rolled his eyes, weariness etched

on his face. "Not this again. I wish you would stop throwing this in my face," he retorted, his voice tinged with defensiveness. "It's my job that supports you and Alicia. If I didn't have it, we wouldn't be living here."

Emotions reached a boiling point, and Sarah felt her patience waning. Taking a deep breath, she attempted to regain composure before speaking words that could irreparably damage their fragile bond. "Damian, I don't know what else to say anymore," she admitted, her voice tinged with resignation. "I know I can't take this arguing anymore."

A flicker of regret crossed Damian's face, his tone softening as he faced the harsh reality. "Well, that's the first thing we've agreed on in a while," he conceded, his voice laced with weariness and a tinge of sadness.

Sarah, her heart heavy with disappointment, met Damian's gaze, her eyes filled with a mix of disbelief and hurt. She shook her head slowly, as if trying to reconcile the person she thought she knew with the one standing before her. "That's your suggestion? Instead of working on everything, you think it would be better to run from your problems?" Her voice quivered with a mix of confusion and disappointment. "I thought I knew you better than this." With those words, she turned and walked out of the kitchen, the weight of their fractured relationship lingering in the air.

$$\infty \infty \infty$$

Chapter 14

The Atkinson household had become a battleground of emotions, its walls bearing witness to the relentless turmoil that had gripped their lives. The shadows of the past loomed large, casting an atmosphere of unease that had seeped into every corner of their once serene abode. Sarah, haunted by the events that had unfolded, had found solace in sleepless nights and restless thoughts, her mind plagued by the fear of what each new day might bring.

With trepidation, she had descended the staircase countless times, her heart pounding in her chest as she approached the kitchen, bracing herself for the unknown. The memories of finding Alicia in that very room, the glint of a menacing knife in her small hand, had etched themselves into Sarah's consciousness - a chilling reminder of the fragility of their daughter's delicate state of mind. The fear of what could have transpired, what dark paths Alicia might have chosen to traverse, weighed heavily upon her soul.

Yet, despite the relentless storm that had raged within their lives, there was a flicker of respite in the air. The passage of time had brought a semblance of calm, like the ebbing of a tempest, leaving behind a fragile tranquility that seemed almost too delicate to trust. Sarah, her eyes heavy with the remnants of sleepless nights, found solace in the sight of the kitchen, no longer a battlefield but a sanctuary of domestic rhythm.

As Sarah stood before the stove, her hands moving with practiced grace, the aroma of home-cooked dinner permeated the air, a symphony of familiar scents that mingled with the lingering tension. The warm embrace of the kitchen enveloped her, its walls seeming to exhale a collective sigh of relief, as if acknowledging the fragile peace that had settled upon their lives.

In that moment, the front door creaked open, signaling Damian's return from a long day at work. Fatigue etched lines upon his face, but his eyes held a softness that only love could ignite. He shed the weight of the outside world, crossing the threshold into the sanctuary of their home, where his wife stood, a pillar of strength and resilience.

The clatter of pots and pans ceased as Sarah turned to face Damian, her eyes alight with a mixture of weariness and affection. His presence, a balm for her weary soul, brought a flicker of hope amidst the lingering doubts that plagued her mind. As he drew near, the touch of his lips against her cheek offered a momentary respite from the relentless storm that had besieged their lives.

"Is Alicia home from school?"

"Yes. I decided after everything that's happened, it's still better that I pick her up. That way I know she'll get home safely," Sarah said.

"How is she?"

"As well as we expected her to be. I did speak to Mr. Avila when I went to pick her up. He wanted to know if there was any change during her suspension. I told him about what happened that night in the kitchen and I told him how we think her problem might be mental."

"What did he have to say about it?"

"He agreed and he was going to pass the word to Mr. Sanders and Mr. Bailey. He'll let me know tomorrow what they suggest is done next."

"That's good. I do think it would be better if we sent her back to Dr. Lyon though. He's more of a professional than the school counselor," Damian said.

"I feel the same way. He may be the one who can get more out of her, especially when we give him the added information of what's happened since the last time he saw her. Oh, there was something else that happened today when I picked her up that surprised me."

"What's that?" Damian was interested.

"She talked about how the school day went. She hasn't done that since this all began. And she didn't mention Shantel."

"Really?" Damian was shocked. "How many days has it been now since she last mentioned her?"

"Three. That's a record for her. And I certainly didn't bring her up either. Damian, do you think that the incident in the kitchen the other day may have been it? You know, the last thing to finally make her get rid of Shantel?"

"It's possible," Damian sat down at the kitchen table. "But I don't want us to get our hopes up. We already thought she moved on from having an imaginary friend before and look how that turned out. I think we need to take everything one step at a time until we find out exactly what is wrong with Alicia."

"You're right. I can't rush something like this." Sarah sat next to her husband. "There's something else that's been on my mind since the morning after the incident. Remember when you brought up us getting a separation?"

Damian shut his eyes, remembering quite

well when he made that suggestion, wishing he didn't. He was talking out of anger about what was going on with Alicia. He and Sarah were married for years and had been through the good and the bad. He never should've mentioned a separation, not when their daughter needed help. And the only way she would get that help was if she had the support of both her parents.

"I am sorry about what I said that morning. I wasn't thinking clearly," he admitted.

"I don't think either of us was thinking clearly," she looked down. "But it hurts that you would even consider us getting a separation. I want us to work together for Alicia's sake."

"And we will," he reached across the table and placed his hands on top of Sarah's hands. "I know we're always going to have our differences on how things should be done and that is fine. We are different people. What's important is that we both want Alicia to get well."

"Yes, of course, that's all I want too. But what does that mean for us?"

Damian squeezed her hands. "We work on our differences and not let it interfere with us getting Alicia the help she needs. I never should've made you feel like you weren't a good mother to her. How could you know what was going on with her when she's so good at hiding everything?

And I'll admit, I haven't been around enough. I'm spending too much time at the dealership. If I'm going to be honest, I think I was spending more hours than I should've because I didn't want to come home and deal with Alicia. For that, I am sorry. I never should've left everything on your shoulders."

"I don't blame you for doing that. Believe me, if I could, I probably would run away instead of having to deal with her. I know we want her to get help, but sometimes I feel like it's more than I can handle and I don't know if I can take it much longer. That is why I agree with you that we need to send her back to Doctor Lyon."

"Let me make a call this afternoon and tell him we want to set up another appointment with him," Damian said. "And sweetheart, I don't want you worrying about this marriage. I won't allow it to fail. We don't know what the future has in store for us as a family, but I do know it's big enough for the both of us to tackle together. I'll do whatever it is I have to for our marriage to survive through the ordeal with Alicia." He got up from the table and kissed Sarah. "I'm going to go upstairs and check on her and let her know dinner is almost ready."

Sarah sat at the table, smiling. Those were the words she needed to hear from her husband, knowing he wasn't planning on ending their marriage. That was one less worry on her mind and now she could focus on the one thing that was important to both of them, Alicia She was glad he was taking charge of making the calls that needed to be done so she could concentrate on their daughter. Soon, this would all be over and they could go on living as a loving family.

****

Later that week, Sarah and Damian brought Alicia to Doctor Lyon. Damian informed him over the phone about the incident in the kitchen and how Alicia said she didn't know why she had the knife in her hand. He also filled him in on the suspension at school due to her bringing a weapon. Doctor Lyon made note of everything Damian told him and when they brought Alicia to his office, he told them he would be spending at least an hour with her and it would be better if they left and came back later.

On the drive back from Doctor Lyon's office, Damian and Sarah talked about how they felt they were finally getting somewhere with Alicia. Doctor Lyon was determined to get Alicia to finally open up to him and Damian and Sarah had hoped this time it would work. And they were going to use this time while Alicia was with the doctor to work on their personal problems.

As Damian pulled up to their house, they noticed a strange man standing in their yard. "Were you expecting anyone today?" he asked

Sarah.

"No. I've never seen that man before."

Damian parked the car and waited for his wife to get out before they walked towards the man on their property. "Excuse me. Can I help you?" He put his arm around Sarah, protecting his wife in case this man was here to harm them.

The guy jumped when he heard Damian. "I'm sorry. I bet you're wondering why I am here."

"You got that right. You do know this is private property you're standing on."

"I do. And I assume you are Damian Atkinson. And this must be your wife, Sarah."

"Who are you?" Damian was growing impatient with this guy ignoring his questions.

"Let me introduce myself. I'm David Cathey and I'm planning on moving to this neighborhood. I was walking around looking for the perfect house to buy and I came upon your house. And I would love to buy it from you. How much would you be willing to sell it to me for? Money's no object. I'll pay anything."

"Who do you think you are?" Sarah pushed away from Damian. "You have some nerve coming onto our property and then think you have the right to ask us to sell our house to you. You are trespassing. We have no idea who you are. On top of everything else, you think it's perfectly normal to ask us to sell our house when clearly there are no signs indicating we're thinking of selling our house."

"Mrs. Atkinson, I understand what you're saying, but don't you see what I'm trying to say? I am willing to offer you and your husband whatever you want for this house. You'll be able to get yourselves a bigger and better house if you sell this house to me. What do you say?"

"I say get off our property before I call the cops. This house is not for sale," Sarah said.

"Now, maybe we should listen more to what he has to say," Damian stopped his wife.

"I said this house isn't for sale," she glared at David. "Get off my property NOW!" Sarah ran inside the house.

Damian apologized to the stranger and ran after his wife. "What was that all about?" He shut the door. "We could've at least discussed it with him."

"Why would we?" Sarah turned to her husband. "I have no desire to sell this house. We moved here wanting to make a better life for Alicia and that's what we're doing."

"Is it? Because look around. Since we

moved here, Alicia hasn't been the same girl we adopted."

"That doesn't mean we have to pack up our things and move, Damian. And don't you think it's kind of strange that this man was here waiting for us so he could try and buy our house? He knew our names. That's kind of scary if you ask me."

"He could've easily found out that information. Our names are on public records as owners of this house. I'll admit it wasn't right for him to be on our property, but there was no need to be rude to him."

Sarah couldn't believe she was having this discussion with her husband. Why would he even consider selling the house? She couldn't talk to him when he was like this.

"Damian, this discussion is over. We are not selling the house and we are not talking to that man. Next time I see him in our yard, I am calling the cops. Is that clear?" She left to go upstairs, needing to get away from her husband.

∞∞∞

Chapter 15

The atmosphere in the house was filled with a mixture of anticipation and apprehension as Sarah and Damian embarked on their mission to restore a sense of normalcy to Alicia's life. However, their efforts were met with disappointment. Despite their hopes, Dr. Lyon's counseling sessions did not yield the desired progress, as Alicia remained closed off and resistant. Her explanation for the incident in the kitchen mirrored the one she had given her parents earlier: a nightmare-induced confusion about how she ended up there. With dwindling options at their disposal, Sarah and Damian clung to the hope that Alicia would eventually overcome this phase.

Descending the stairs into the living room, Damian sought confirmation that everything was in order. The room was occupied by a small gathering of Alicia's friends from her previous school. Meanwhile, Sarah emerged from the kitchen, carefully balancing a tray of snacks in her hands.

"I texted Alicia to inform her that I won't be able to pick her up from school," Sarah announced, placing the delectable treats on the table. "Damian, I'm starting to question whether throwing this surprise party was the right decision. I hate not being there to pick her up."

"Sarah, we agreed that we need to reintroduce normalcy into her life, even if it means allowing her to come home from school on her own," Damian reassured her. "And imagine how thrilled she'll be when she arrives home and discovers this surprise party we've organized for her. It was a brilliant idea to bring her friends from the city back here to celebrate."

"You're right," Sarah forced a smile, her worries temporarily assuaged. "The school hasn't contacted us about any issues, so maybe things are finally settling down." Just as Sarah uttered these words, her phone emitted a familiar beep, notifying her of a text message from Alicia.

Alicia: Walking home now.

Sarah: See you soon, birthday girl. Love you!

"Girls, Alicia will be home in about fifteen minutes. When she walks through that door, we'll shout 'Surprise!'" Sarah glanced back at her phone, hoping for a response from Alicia, but none had arrived.

"Is everything okay?" Damian, sensing his wife's disappointment, approached her from behind.

"Yes," Sarah quickly brushed away her momentary letdown. "I guess I shouldn't have expected her to respond to my text with 'love you.' She's never said those words to us before. Why would she start now? Just wishful thinking, I suppose."

"Wait until she sees the party you've organized. How could she not be overjoyed?" Damian offered reassurance as he leaned in to plant a tender kiss on Sarah's cheek.

"I hope you're right," Sarah sighed, her hopes riding on the success of the surprise gathering. Suddenly, the sound of the front door being unlocked resonated throughout the house. "Everyone, she's here!" Sarah exclaimed, her voice filled with excitement.

As Alicia pushed the door open and stepped into the living room, she was immediately engulfed by a chorus of shrill voices exclaiming, "SURPRISE!" The unexpected commotion jolted her, causing her to momentarily lose her balance. "What's happening? Why are they here?" Alicia's eyes darted nervously around the room, her enthusiasm noticeably absent at the sight of her old school friends.

"Sweetie, it's your birthday," Damian

approached his daughter, attempting to bridge the gap between her confusion and the celebration. "Your mother went back to your old school and brought some of your friends here to celebrate with us."

Sarah joined in, embracing her daughter tightly. "Are you surprised?" she asked, her voice tinged with a mix of hope and concern, yearning for a glimmer of joy to illuminate Alicia's face.

Alicia's anger burned within her, intensifying with each passing moment. The prospect of spending the next few hours with people she hadn't seen in over a year ignited her frustration. Once her friends, they now felt like distant figures from a previous chapter of her life. She longed for solitude, for a chance to escape this forced reunion and embrace her new existence. Her parents needed to comprehend that she had moved on, that her life had taken a different trajectory.

"We understand that this past year has been challenging for you, with the transition to a new school in a new town. I thought it would be a wonderful birthday surprise," Sarah explained, her voice tinged with a hint of pleading.

"Well, I hate it!" Alicia's voice trembled with resentment. "I have things to do after school, and now I have to spend time with these girls whom I no longer consider my friends." She shook her head in frustration, her desire to flee suppressed by the reality of the situation. "Fine, I'll join the party, but I want you to know that I'm not happy about this."

Exhausted and disheartened, Sarah raised her hands in surrender. "I give up. I try to do something nice for her, and she hates me. I should have known this plan would backfire."

"Nothing she does should come as a surprise to us," Damian chimed in, his voice laced with resignation. "At least she's in the living room. Why don't you bring out the pizza for everyone? I'll keep an eye on how she interacts with the girls. The sooner the party is over, the better."

"True," Sarah agreed, her voice tinged with a mix of resignation and determination. "How much trouble could she get into while we're here?" She chuckled softly, making her way into the kitchen. Within seconds, she returned, balancing a tray of fragrant pizza in her hands. "Who wants pizza?"

The girls eagerly descended upon the table, clamoring to grab a slice for themselves. However, Alicia remained seated on the couch, a sullen expression etched upon her face. Sarah refused to give up on her mission to brighten her daughter's special day. Determined, she selected a slice of pizza and approached Alicia. "You must be hungry," she offered, her voice filled with a mix of concern and hope.

"I'm not," Alicia replied curtly, her response laced with defiance.

"Alicia, please, I'm trying my best here," Sarah implored, her desperation evident. "I planned this party because I thought you deserved something good after the chaos of the past five months. What more do you want from me?"

"You want to know what I want?" Alicia's voice dripped with frustration. "I want you and Dad to leave me alone once and for all! That's what I want! Today, I had plans to retreat to my room, to have time for myself. I never wanted this stupid party, but now I'm stuck down here because you invited all these girls whom I no longer connect with. And you keep sending me to Doctor Lyon, even though I refuse to speak to him! Next time, before you plan another party for me, consider how I'll feel about it first."

"Alicia..." Sarah began, her voice tinged with a mix of remorse and understanding.

"Stop. Just stop," Alicia interrupted, her voice filled with a mix of frustration and anguish. Determination welled up within her as she rose from the couch, her resolve unyielding. "I'm going upstairs to my room. I want no part in this party."

"Can't you just stay down here and wait for the cake?" Sarah pleaded, a glimmer of hope lingering in her voice. "Your father went to pick it up from the bakery, and he should be back soon."

"Do I even have a choice?" Alicia snapped, her annoyance palpable.

Sarah rose from her seat, her heart heavy with concern, and made her way to check on the other girls. Alicia's rejection and disdain pierced her deeply, casting a shadow of regret over the entire party. Despite her efforts, Sarah couldn't shake the feeling that nothing she did could bring back the vibrant, joyful girl they had adopted. She mourned the loss of the person Alicia had become since their move to this unfamiliar town.

Just as the atmosphere seemed to grow heavier, a glimmer of excitement filled the air as Damian entered the house, proudly announcing his return with the cake in hand.

"CAKE!" The girls erupted in a chorus of gleeful screams, congregating around the table like bees drawn to nectar.

"Alicia, come take your place at the table," Sarah called out, her voice carrying a mix of hope and apprehension. She walked into the kitchen, assisting Damian in placing the candles atop the cake.

"What did I miss while I was gone?" Damian inquired, his curiosity piqued.

"Well, Alicia made it abundantly clear how

she feels about the party. She pretty much told me she despises it and wants the two of us to stay out of her life. In other words, you didn't miss much because she's still exhibiting the same behavior," Sarah replied, a tinge of sadness lacing her words.

"Perhaps her attitude will change once she lays eyes on the cake," Damian suggested optimistically, a warm smile gracing his face as he lit the candles.

Sarah ventured into the dining room, flicking off the lights to create an ambiance of celebration. Meanwhile, Damian emerged, carrying the cake with care, gently setting it down on the table. The moment to sing "Happy Birthday" was on the horizon when suddenly, Alicia rose from her seat, forcefully shoving her plate off the table.

"WHAT DO YOU THINK YOU'RE DOING WITH THIS CAKE?" Alicia's voice reverberated with anger, her eyes ablaze with fury.

Confusion and concern danced across Sarah's face as she attempted to maintain an air of calm. "Alicia, what's wrong?" she inquired, her voice steady and composed.

"Do you think this is some kind of joke?" Alicia seethed, her frustration evident to all.

The room fell into a bewildered silence as everyone exchanged perplexed glances. Sarah and

Damian, at a loss for words, glanced at each other, searching for answers. Damian took a step forward, attempting to soothe Alicia's escalating rage.

"Alicia, what are you talking about? This is your birthday cake. It's not a joke. We got chocolate, your favorite," he reasoned, his voice laced with a gentle plea.

"WOULD YOU STOP CALLING ME THAT? YOU CAN'T EVEN GET MY NAME RIGHT ON THE CAKE!" Alicia's voice trembled with fury, her words lashing out like a venomous serpent.

Damian's gaze shifted to the cake, searching for the mistake Alicia had pointed out. However, his eyes found nothing amiss. Confusion clouded his features as he turned to Sarah, seeking understanding.

"Do you know what she's talking about?" he whispered, his voice tinged with a mix of concern and bewilderment.

"I have no idea," Sarah admitted, her eyes scanning the cake in search of any errors. "It says, 'Happy Birthday Alicia.'"

"THAT'S WHAT I'M TALKING ABOUT! MY NAME ISN'T ALICIA! IT'S SHANTEL! GET IT RIGHT!" Alicia's scream echoed through the room, her outburst leaving everyone stunned and silenced.

The weight of the revelation hung heavily in the air as Sarah, Damian, and the guests attempted to process the magnitude of Alicia's outburst. The realization that they had been calling her by the wrong name struck like a thunderbolt, unraveling the delicate thread of understanding that had held the family together.

"I am so sorry about that," Sarah apologized to the bewildered guests, her voice tinged with a mix of regret and embarrassment. "Please, help yourselves to some cake. I'll personally drive each of you home." Her words carried a sincere promise of restitution, a small attempt to salvage the remnants of what was meant to be a joyous celebration.

After a long and emotionally exhausting evening, Sarah finally returned home, having driven each of the girls back to their respective houses. As she stepped through the front door, she found Damian seated in the living room, his face etched with worry.

"Has she come down from her room?" Sarah inquired, her voice heavy with concern.

"No," Damian replied, his tone tinged with frustration. "I've tried going up to check on her, but she refuses to let me in. Every time I call her Alicia, she yells at me. It was one thing when she had Shantel as an imaginary friend, but now she's taken it to a new level, demanding that we call her Shantel."

Sarah slumped down on the couch next to her husband, a mixture of fear and sadness consuming her. "That outburst she had really scared me," she confessed, her voice trembling.

"Perhaps it's been building up inside her for months, and today was the breaking point," Damian offered, his voice filled with a mix of understanding and uncertainty. "You did mention how much she despised the idea of this party. Maybe that's what pushed her over the edge."

"I should've known this party was a terrible idea, but I kept pushing forward with the planning," Sarah lamented, tears streaming down her face. "What if it's my fault that she reached her breaking point?"

Damian gently lifted Sarah's tear-streaked face, looking into her eyes with a comforting gaze. "Listen to me," he began, his voice filled with reassurance. "Something is clearly wrong with Alicia. We both know that. We can't predict what might trigger her outbursts. What happened tonight was frightening. What we don't know is whether this is all an act or if she genuinely believes that Shantel is a part of her now. We must discuss this with Dr. Lyon during our next appointment."

"But what if we can't even get Alicia to go see him? She told me that seeing the doctor isn't helping, and deep down, I have a feeling she might be right," Sarah murmured, her voice laden with worry.

Damian wrapped his arms around his wife, providing her with a comforting embrace. "I understand your concerns. We've both been through a lot today, especially after Alicia's outburst during the party. Right now, neither of us is thinking clearly. Let's go upstairs, check on our daughter, and then take some time for ourselves. We need a couple of days to process what happened and figure out the best course of action."

Sarah nodded in agreement, finding solace in Damian's words. "That sounds like a good plan," she replied, rising from the couch. "We need some space to reflect on everything that has transpired and determine our next steps."

Together, they ascended the stairs, their footsteps hushed with trepidation. As they reached Alicia's door, they peered inside, their hearts skipping a beat. The sight of their daughter peacefully asleep brought them a momentary sense of relief. With a shared sigh, they retreated to their own bedroom, acutely aware of the urgency to address whatever was ailing their daughter before her behavior spiraled further out of control.

∞ ∞ ∞

Chapter 16

The weight of unease hung heavy in the air, casting a veil of apprehension over their once peaceful home. The remnants of the ill-fated birthday party lingered, like shadows of a distorted reality that had unfolded before their eyes. Damian and Sarah, their faces etched with worry and disbelief, sought solace in each other's presence, their fingers interlaced as they walked out of Alicia's room.

The hallway seemed narrower, suffocating, as if echoing the confines of their own thoughts. Damian's arm encircled Sarah's trembling frame, offering a feeble attempt at reassurance amidst the turmoil that had consumed their lives. The weight of the situation pressed upon them, their footsteps heavy with the burden of a decision that could no longer be postponed.

As they stood at the threshold of their daughter's room, it felt as though the walls themselves held secrets—a space that had once exuded innocence and joy now harbored the darkness of an alternate reality. The remnants of the once-celebratory decorations hung limply, their vibrant colors fading into a muted palette of unease. The toys and games scattered about seemed to taunt them, reminders of the unsettling presence that had infiltrated their daughter's mind.

Damian's voice broke the silence, his words laced with a mixture of concern and determination. "We need to talk about this," he said, his voice carrying the weight of a decision that had long been postponed.

Sarah nodded, her eyes reflecting a mixture of weariness and resolve. She understood the gravity of the situation, the urgent need to address the turmoil that had enveloped their daughter's young mind. With a silent understanding, they turned away from Alicia's room, leaving behind the remnants of shattered innocence, and made their way downstairs.

The kitchen, once a haven of domestic tranquility, now bore witness to their shared anguish. Damian took a seat at the worn, wooden table, his gaze drifting back to Alicia's room once more, his heart heavy with worry. Sarah moved with purpose, her steps measured as she prepared the life-giving elixir of coffee, seeking solace in its warmth and familiarity.

She placed the steaming mugs on the

table, the comforting aroma filling the space, intertwining with the tension that hung thick in the air. As they sat side by side, their hands finding each other's in a desperate search for support, the silence between them grew pregnant with unspoken words, an uncharted territory they were about to traverse.

The first sip of coffee brought a fleeting moment of respite, the rich, bittersweet taste providing a fleeting distraction from the weight of their shared burden. Their gazes met, seeking solace and strength in each other's eyes, yet both hesitating to broach the difficult conversation that lay before them.

The room seemed to hold its breath, the air heavy with anticipation, as they struggled to find the right words. The ticking of the clock on the wall became an unwelcome reminder of the passage of time, urging them to confront the truth that had been thrust upon them.

Finally, with a deep breath, Sarah mustered the courage to break the silence. Her voice, though tinged with vulnerability, carried a determination that mirrored her love for their daughter.

"We can't ignore this any longer," she began, her voice steady yet laced with a thread of desperation. "Alicia needs our help, professional help. We can't let her face this alone."

Damian nodded, his grip on Sarah's hand tightening in agreement. The weight of responsibility settled upon their shoulders, a shared burden that they knew they had to shoulder together.

"We'll find the right resources, the right support," Damian vowed, his voice a pledge of unwavering commitment. "We'll do everything we can to help our daughter find her way back to us."

In that moment, their eyes locked in a shared resolve, they took solace in the unity that their love provided. The path ahead may be fraught with challenges, but they were determined to navigate it together, armed with love, perseverance, and the unwavering belief that their daughter's journey to healing and happiness would be guided by their unwavering support.

Leaving Alicia's room, Damian instinctively wrapped his arm around Sarah for support as they walked into the hallway. Sensing the weight of the situation, he voiced his concern. "We need to address this," he said softly.

"You're right. After what happened tonight, I doubt we'll get much sleep. I'll go make some coffee," Sarah replied, her voice filled with worry.

Damian let out a sigh, casting one last glance at his daughter's room before making his way downstairs. He settled at the kitchen table, and soon Sarah joined him, placing the mugs of coffee on the table. In silence, they both took a sip, bracing themselves for the difficult conversation ahead.

Finally, Sarah broke the silence. "What do you make of all this? I mean, we knew she had been talking about Shantel for months, but for her to claim that as her name now... it's terrifying."

"It goes beyond a mere imaginary friend," Damian responded, his voice tinged with concern. "What baffles me is how she conjured up this person in the first place."

"And those specialists she's seen haven't been of any help either. All they said was to encourage her and play along. Look where that's gotten us," Sarah added, frustration evident in her voice. She turned to Damian. "What's our next step?"

Damian shook his head, feeling helpless in the face of their daughter's inexplicable behavior. "I don't think talking to Alicia directly will yield any answers. We need to delve into the origins of Shantel, but now that Alicia believes it's her own name, she won't provide us with any information."

Sarah tapped her nails on the table, lost in thought until a sudden realization struck her. "Wait. I might have an idea."

"You do?" Damian asked, surprised.

"I'm not sure if it will work, but with everything that's been happening, I completely forgot what the realtor told us about this house when we moved in. About the girl who was murdered here. You know how they say strange things can occur in places where murders took place? What if that's what's affecting Alicia?"

"Sarah, you can't seriously believe this place is haunted, can you?" Damian questioned, skepticism lacing his words.

"Stranger things have happened before. And it would explain the sudden change in Alicia. Do you remember anything else Thomas mentioned about the murder?"

Damian scrunched his face in thought, then shook his head. "Honestly, I tuned him out as soon as he handed over the keys. I was just happy we finally found a new home. But from what I recall, he did mention that a family lived here fifty years ago, and their daughter was kidnapped while playing in the front yard. They found her lifeless body miles away."

Sarah jotted down notes, her face determined. "Tomorrow, while you're at work, I'll do some research and find out more about what happened in this house. Maybe I can uncover some information that will shed light on why Alicia is behaving this way."

"Alright, that sounds like a plan." Damian rose from his seat and took the coffee mugs, depositing them in the sink. "Let's try to get some sleep. Tomorrow is going to be a busy day."

****

The following morning, Sarah awoke with a resolute determination to dive into her research. The idea that had sparked in her mind the previous night echoed loudly, compelling her to take action. There was an urgency to her mission, a sense that time was running out, and she couldn't bear to contemplate the potential consequences if they didn't intervene soon enough to help Alicia.

Making her way downstairs to the kitchen, Sarah discovered Alicia sitting at the table, idly toying with the breakfast Damian had prepared. She attempted to maintain a facade of normalcy, despite the unsettling events of the previous day.

"Good morning, Alicia. Is something wrong? Not hungry today?" Sarah asked, her voice laced with concern.

Alicia glanced up from her plate, a disdainful sneer etched across her face. "I told you, my name is Shantel. I don't know who Alicia is," she retorted. "To answer your question, no, I'm not hungry. I don't understand why he," she pointed an accusatory finger at Damian, "gave me this. I've never eaten it before."

"Firstly, you will not refer to me as 'him.' I am your father," Damian interjected, his voice tinged with a mix of frustration and paternal authority. However, Sarah raised a hand to halt his response.

"Damian, remember, we don't fully comprehend what's happening inside her mind. We mustn't be too hard on her," Sarah reminded him gently. Turning her attention back to Alicia, she continued, "I apologize. I forgot. But your father is right; he is your father. And this used to be your favorite breakfast."

"Well, it's not anymore," Alicia declared, pushing the plate away. "I'm going to school, and I don't want either of you following me there." With that, she swiftly grabbed her coat and backpack, and without further ado, she left.

"Sarah, I won't be going to work today. I'll accompany you in your quest to uncover what happened on the day of that girl's murder," Damian stated. He was resolute in his decision not to let his wife shoulder the burden alone.

****

The couple embarked on their quest by reaching out to the neighbors, hoping to gather information about the fateful day of the murder. Regrettably, the passage of fifty years had caused most of the original residents to move away, leaving behind no trace of their whereabouts. Even the parents of the murdered girl had departed, driven by the lack of conviction for the killer, vanishing into obscurity. The Riggs, the family in question, had seemingly vanished as well, leaving Sarah and Damian uncertain of their current existence. Frustration and hopelessness crept into Sarah's heart as their efforts led them back to square one, devoid of any valuable leads.

"Sarah, there's still one avenue we haven't explored," Damian proposed, his voice tinged with a glimmer of optimism. "While the neighbors may be unwilling to share information, a news story of such magnitude cannot remain concealed forever."

Confusion and despondency clouded Sarah's voice as she responded, "What do you mean? We've spent the entire day going from house to house, and no one has been willing to assist us."

"That only proves that relying on individuals might not yield results. However, we can trust in the records and reports surrounding the incident," Damian explained, a smile tugging at the corners of his lips. "And where better to find such information than the public library? They are likely to have archived newspapers from that time. What do you think?"

A flicker of hope ignited within Sarah as she considered her husband's suggestion. "You're right. Instead of standing here, we should be at the library. Let's go!"

"Now you're speaking my language!"

Damian and Sarah made their way to the car and set off towards the library. The drive was brief, as the entire town was conveniently within walking distance. However, with each passing moment, Sarah's heart pounded against her ribcage, the proximity to the library intensifying her anticipation. At long last, after months of agonizing uncertainty, she and her husband were on the verge of uncovering the truth behind their daughter's mysterious behavior and the events that had transpired within their own home.

Entering the library, they made their way to the research room, where an extensive collection of newspapers was housed. "Let's divide and conquer," Damian suggested, observing the stacks of papers that awaited them. "Between the two of us, we'll gather all the information we need."

Damian and Sarah diligently gathered as many newspapers as they could from the time of the murder and settled at a table in the room. Damian held a stack of twenty papers, while Sarah managed to uncover around thirty, leaving Damian astounded by her findings.

"I had no idea we would stumble upon such a wealth of information," he admitted, his voice tinged with awe.

"I suppose when a murder rocks a quiet town, the news reverberates throughout the surrounding areas," Sarah mused, taking her seat at the table. "We should start reading these articles if we want to finish before Alicia returns from school."

Hours drifted away as they immersed themselves in the accounts of the murder day, meticulously examining interviews with the neighbors. It was during this exhaustive search that Sarah stumbled upon an article that sent a shiver down her spine. Her face turned pale, and she repeated the word "no" in disbelief.

Concern etched on his features, Damian

inquired, "Honey, what's wrong?" His worry grew as he witnessed his wife's deteriorating condition.

Handing him the article, Sarah whispered, "Read it. It's about the little girl who was murdered. She was adopted, just like Alicia. And look at the name. Shantel."

Damian's trembling hands held the article as he absorbed its contents. Shantel had been ten years old, the exact age their daughter had been when they had adopted her and moved to this very town. The uncanny similarities between the two girls sent a chill down his spine.

"D-Damian?" Sarah attempted to regain her husband's attention, her voice quivering. "Damian?"

"I'm sorry," he replied, placing the article down. "It's just... It hits too close to home. I mean, what are the odds that we would move into the very house where she was killed?"

"And the name, Damian. Shantel. How could Alicia possibly know about her? We never disclosed the fact that a murder had occurred in our home," Sarah lamented.

"Do you think she found out from someone else?" Damian posed the question, searching for answers.

"Who, Damian? She hardly leaves the house, except to go to school. Yet somehow, she learned about Shantel. Unless... never mind," Sarah dismissed a fleeting thought, her anxiety evident.

"I'm letting my imagination run wild again. I've watched one too many horror movies," she chuckled nervously, masking her unease.

Damian surveyed the growing crowd in the research room, prompting him to pull out his phone and discreetly capture photographs of the article. "I think it would be best for us to discuss this at home, where we can be alone. These pictures of the article will prove useful since we can't take the newspapers with us," he suggested, gently taking hold of his wife's hand and helping her rise from her chair. "Let's go home."

Sarah fought back tears as they drove back, but the floodgates opened, and she couldn't contain her emotions. Her worry for Alicia had escalated to new heights, overshadowing any previous concerns. "What is happening to my little girl?" she sobbed. "I just want our adopted daughter back."

Damian sighed, stealing glances at his distraught wife as he pulled into the driveway. It was becoming increasingly challenging for him to maintain composure after the revelations at the library. Nevertheless, he knew that one of them had to remain strong. Wrapping his arm around Sarah, he murmured, "We'll get through this. I promise."

"Damian, I want to believe you. I really do. But I'm terrified that something is seriously wrong with Alicia. What if this is beyond our control?" Sarah confessed her deepest fears.

"I share your concerns. It's time we accept that she needs professional help," Damian suggested, his voice laced with conviction. "Someone who can truly delve into her mind and unravel what's going on."

"But who? The counselors haven't been able to provide any solutions. They keep attributing her behavior to the move and leaving her old friends behind," Sarah lamented.

"I believe it's time to consider a psychiatrist. Someone who can offer the expertise and insight we need. Professional help may be the only way to reach our daughter," Damian proposed, determined to explore all avenues.

Sarah nodded, her tears subsiding momentarily. "You're right. We owe it to Alicia to seek the help she requires. It's time to take that step."

As they stood united in their decision, Sarah and Damian prepared themselves for the difficult journey ahead, bracing for the unknown as they sought solace and answers for their troubled daughter.

$$\infty\infty\infty$$

Chapter 17

Sarah and Damian dedicated the entire morning to their search for a suitable psychiatrist who could provide the necessary assistance for their daughter, Alicia. The issue they were facing with Alicia was extremely grave and delicate, so they wanted to ensure that they selected someone who would show empathy towards their problem and possess the ability to offer effective help.

Their online exploration led them to discover Ann Barnes, a psychiatrist who specialized in working with children who had endured traumatic experiences. Considering Alicia's challenging upbringing prior to her adoption, they were well aware that her life had never been easy. After reading several reviews about Ann Barnes, they felt confident that she was the right professional to reach out to Alicia and liberate her from whatever grip was holding her.

Filled with hope, Damian dialed the phone number listed on Ann Barnes' website, eagerly anticipating the possibility of securing an appointment for Alicia as soon as possible.

"Hello, this is Doctor Barnes' office. How may I assist you?" responded the secretary on the other end.

"Doctor Barnes? Hi, my name is Damian Atkinson. I came across your name online. My wife and I are in search of a psychiatrist for our daughter. She's ten years old, but she's been going through something that has us completely stumped. We've had her speak with counselors both at school and elsewhere, but unfortunately, they haven't been able to provide us with any solutions. Initially, we believed she was merely referring to an imaginary friend she had created, but now she wants to be addressed by the name of this friend. I understand that what I'm saying may sound nonsensical, but we're at a loss as to where else to turn," Damian explained, his nervousness palpable in his voice.

"Sir, I want you to take a deep breath and try to remain calm. I understand your concerns, and I believe it would be best to discuss this matter in person. The earliest appointment I have available for your daughter is at four o'clock today. Would that be suitable for you? Given the information you've shared, I believe the sooner we address this, the better," responded the secretary, her tone soothing and reassuring.

"Today?" Damian glanced over at his wife and flashed a thumbs-up sign. "Yes, that's perfect. We will pick her up from school and bring her over this afternoon. Thank you, Doctor. We genuinely appreciate you accommodating us on such short notice. Thank you," he expressed his gratitude before hanging up the phone. Turning to Sarah, he exclaimed, "Sarah, we have an appointment for today. It seems like we are finally making progress."

The couple felt a renewed sense of optimism and relief upon securing the appointment, as they believed they were now taking significant steps towards helping their daughter.

****

Alicia seethed in the backseat of the car, her arms tightly crossed, her anger directed at her parents for picking her up from school against her wishes. She had insisted on walking home, but they had overruled her and insisted she accompany them. As they drove through the familiar streets, Alicia's growing frustration turned into panic when she realized her father was taking a different route.

"Where are you taking me? Why aren't we going home? Help! Help! You're kidnapping me!" she screamed frantically, her voice filled with fear and desperation.

Damian and Sarah tried to remain composed, determined to stay focused on their mission. They exchanged glances, silently acknowledging the difficulty of the situation, but they remained resolute in their decision. Ignoring Alicia's pleas, Damian continued driving until they reached Doctor Barnes' office.

When they arrived, Doctor Barnes was waiting for them outside the office. She extended her hand and warmly greeted the Atkinson couple. "Mr. and Mrs. Atkinson, it's a pleasure to meet you. And you must be Alicia," she said, looking directly at the girl.

"I don't know what they told you about me, but my name is Shantel. And why am I here?" Alicia retorted, her voice defiant and tinged with suspicion.

"Alicia, Doctor Barnes is here to help you," Sarah interjected gently, attempting to diffuse the tension.

"I don't need any help," Alicia snapped, her voice dripping with defiance and frustration.

Doctor Barnes, undeterred by Alicia's resistance, remained calm and composed. "I'll just bring her inside my office. You both can stay for the time being. I want to use today as an opportunity to get to know Alicia better before we decide on further sessions," she explained, gesturing for Alicia to follow her.

Reluctantly, Alicia followed the doctor into her office. She slumped down in the chair, her face etched with a scowl, arms still defiantly crossed. "Look, just get to whatever you want to talk about. You're wasting my time. I have important things to do," she grumbled, her voice laced with annoyance.

"Do you? Why don't you tell me about the

things you have to do? I might be able to help," Doctor Barnes responded, her tone gentle and inquisitive.

"Honestly, I highly doubt that. No one has been able to help me before. This is something I have to figure out on my own," Alicia retorted, her voice filled with skepticism and a touch of vulnerability.

"I understand that you don't want to be here, but your parents are genuinely concerned about you," the doctor empathetically acknowledged.

Alicia shrugged dismissively. "So what? I've told them there's nothing to worry about. All I want is for them to stay out of my business once and for all!"

Taking notes as Alicia spoke, Doctor Barnes paused and put her notepad down. "From what I understand, you're expressing that your parents don't understand you," she summarized, her eyes fixed on Alicia.

Alicia shook her head. "No. What I'm saying is that they need to let me live my life once and for all. They need to stop trying to figure me out. Even now, they didn't ask if I wanted to come here and talk to you. They just picked me up from school and brought me here. Can I go now?" Her words were filled with a mix of frustration, vulnerability, and a longing for freedom.

Doctor Barnes sighed softly, realizing the depth of Alicia's resistance and the layers of pain she was concealing. "I believe I've heard enough from you for now. This session is over," she declared, her voice tinged with a mixture of compassion and determination. She walked Alicia out of her office and into the lobby, where Damian anxiously awaited an update.

"Doctor Barnes, how did it go?" Damian inquired, his voice filled with concern and hope.

"I couldn't get too much out of her today, but this initial meeting was crucial for me to begin understanding Alicia on a deeper level. There are underlying issues that are deeply rooted in her psyche, and it will take several more sessions before I can determine the best course of action. I would like to schedule an appointment for next week, and from there, we'll assess how many additional sessions will be necessary," Doctor Barnes explained thoughtfully, her gaze shifting between Alicia's parents.

"Yes, doctor. We're willing to do whatever it takes to get our daughter the help she needs," Damian affirmed, his voice filled with a mix of determination and genuine concern.

As they left the office, Sarah and Damian felt a glimmer of hope. Although the road ahead remained uncertain, they were determined to support Alicia through her journey of healing and self-discovery.

****

A week later, Alicia sat in the car, letting out

a series of moans and groans as her parents drove her back to Doctor Barnes' office. She couldn't believe they were doing this to her again. She had pleaded with them, insisting that she didn't need a psychiatrist and begging them not to bring her back. Yet, here she was, trapped in the car on her way to another meeting she had no desire to attend.

Upon their arrival, Doctor Barnes greeted the Atkinson family and led Alicia directly to her office. Despite the passage of time, Alicia's demeanor remained unchanged from their initial meeting. Her arms were crossed defiantly, and her eyes rolled dismissively at everything the doctor said. However, Doctor Barnes was not one to easily give up. She had made a promise to Alicia's parents that she would help their daughter, and she intended to keep it.

"Alicia, please, I implore you to listen to what I'm saying. I am only trying to help you," Doctor Barnes spoke gently, her voice filled with empathy. "But I cannot assist you if you refuse to answer my questions."

"It's Shantel," Alicia mumbled under her breath.

"I'm sorry, what was that?" Doctor Barnes leaned in, her concern evident.

"I said, it's Shantel. That's my name. You keep calling me Alicia."

Doctor Barnes glanced down at the papers

Damian and Sarah had provided her, her brows furrowing in worry that she may have been using the wrong name all along. "You're saying your name is Shantel?"

"Yes, that's right. Why? What does it say on those papers?" Alicia's fingers tapped impatiently on the armrest of the chair, her gaze shifting towards the clock on the wall. How much longer until she could escape this place?

"Your parents told me your name is Alicia Atkinson," Doctor Barnes replied, her voice tinged with surprise.

Alicia let out a bitter laugh. "Of course they would lie to you. They refuse to acknowledge that my name is Shantel. I have been insisting that they call me by my real name, but they insist on calling me Alicia," she said, rolling her eyes in frustration. "I shouldn't be surprised. My birth parents didn't want me, and now these adoptive parents of mine don't listen to a word I say. I should have seen this coming."

Doctor Barnes had been aware that Alicia was adopted, but she had not realized the extent to which the girl remembered her early experiences and the treatment she had received from her birth parents. Sensing an opportunity to delve deeper into Alicia's past, the doctor gently probed, "Please, tell me more about what you remember of your life before the Atkinsons adopted you."

****

An hour later, Doctor Barnes emerged from her office and stepped into the waiting room. "Mr. and Mrs. Atkinson, could you please come into my office? I'd like to talk to the two of you for a moment," she requested, motioning for them to follow her. Alicia remained in the waiting room, her apprehension palpable.

Once inside the office, Sarah nervously took a seat, her gaze fixed on Doctor Barnes. "What is it, Doctor?" she asked, her voice tinged with concern.

"I had a very interesting discussion with Alicia," Doctor Barnes began, her tone measured. "She still insists on being called Shantel. She won't tell me why, but she claims that's her name."

Damian interjected, his voice filled with a mix of confusion and alarm. "About that... We recently discovered that a family who lived in our house fifty years ago had a daughter named Shantel. Tragically, she was kidnapped while playing on the front lawn and found murdered a few days later. However, we never shared that story with Alicia, so we're at a loss as to how she found out."

"I'll try to delve further into that matter during our future sessions. Today, she also brought up her life before you adopted her. Do you have any information about that?" Doctor Barnes inquired, her curiosity piqued.

Sarah took a deep breath, her gaze unfocused as she recalled Alicia's troubled past. "She was abandoned by her birth parents at a very young age. From there, she endured a series of challenging experiences, being shuffled from one foster home to another until we finally adopted her last year," she explained, her voice laden with empathy.

Doctor Barnes nodded, her astute gaze fixed on the couple. "Everything is starting to fall into place. While I'm still uncertain as to why she insists on being called Shantel, I believe Alicia is grappling with intense and profound mental episodes rooted in the trauma she experienced when her birth parents abandoned her. It seems she may be experiencing vivid flashbacks and descending into states of deep depression," she revealed, her voice filled with compassion.

Sarah's eyes widened with concern. "Do you think this is connected to the whole Shantel situation? When she demanded that Damian and I start calling her by that name, it truly frightened us."

"I understand your worries, and I assure you that I will do everything within my power to uncover the truth," Doctor Barnes reassured them. "However, we must proceed with caution, taking one step at a time."

Damian leaned forward, his voice laced with apprehension. "What do you suggest we do next?"

"As I mentioned before, today's session has confirmed that I need to continue working with Alicia. I cannot determine the exact number of sessions required at this stage, but I have a strong intuition that eventually, she will begin to open up to me. Additionally, I will prescribe medication to help alleviate her depressive episodes. Rest assured, the medication is suitable for her, and while it won't be overpowering, it should provide the necessary support during these difficult moments," Doctor Barnes explained, her tone steady and reassuring.

Sarah let out a sigh of relief, gratitude evident in her voice. "And you believe that it's depression that's causing her to display these behaviors?"

"Yes, I do. Depression can manifest in various ways, and although you claim not to have shared the story of the previous family with Alicia, she may have learned about it from another source. With further sessions, I hope to uncover the truth," Doctor Barnes replied, her conviction unwavering.

Sarah's eyes welled up with tears as she spoke, her voice filled with genuine appreciation. "Doctor, I cannot express enough how grateful we are for everything you're doing to help our daughter. It means the world to us."

∞ ∞ ∞

Chapter 18

The meeting with Dr. Barnes had left Sarah and Damian feeling somewhat relieved, although they still lacked a direct answer regarding Alicia's peculiar behavior and her insistence on being called Shantel. Nevertheless, they were one step closer to understanding that Alicia was grappling with depression.

That evening at dinner, Alicia expressed her discontent by pushing her plate away after barely touching her food. Sensing her daughter's distress, Sarah looked to Damian, hoping he could find the right words to address the situation. "Alicia, you're not upset about us taking you to Dr. Barnes, are you?" Damian inquired.

"It's Shantel," Alicia retorted, her annoyance evident. "Can I go to my room?"

"I'm sorry. You're right. I forgot. We were hoping we could have a family discussion," Damian acknowledged. He and Sarah had decided that a heartfelt conversation was necessary, particularly after hearing what Dr. Barnes had revealed.

Alicia scoffed, exasperated. "You must be kidding me. I've had enough talking with that doctor. By the way, you're wasting your money on her. She doesn't know a thing about me and only pretends to care."

"Sweetie, the reason we want you to see Dr. Barnes is because we're genuinely concerned about you," Sarah interjected. "And that's precisely why your father and I have come up with a wonderful idea. Damian, why don't you tell her?"

"We know you've been going through a lot lately, especially with us uprooting you from your previous school and friends to move here. We want to make things better. What's one thing you truly desire?" Damian asked, his voice filled with empathy.

Alicia's frustration boiled over. "For the two of you to leave me alone? That's what I've been telling you for months. I want to be left to my own devices so I can do what I need to do, but you guys keep interfering."

"That's not what we mean, Alicia." Damian and Sarah decided to address her by her real name, refusing to yield to her demand of being called Shantel. "Since you didn't enjoy the surprise birthday party we planned for you, we want to get you a birthday present that you genuinely want. What's something significant that you've been yearning for? Just tell me, and I'll go and get it."

Alicia slammed her fists on the table, her frustration palpable. "Nothing! I want you to let me go so I can retreat to my room and attend to matters that require my attention."

"What is it that you need to do that can't wait a few minutes while we talk?" Damian inquired. "Your homework can wait. This is important."

"No! What's important is the secret project I'm working on, and both of you keep preventing me from pursuing it. I can't take it anymore! Now, if you don't mind, I'm leaving," Alicia declared, ready to rise from her seat. However, Sarah's tears halted her in her tracks.

"Alicia, we're only trying to help. But how can we assist you when you refuse to communicate with us? Every time we attempt to talk to you, you find an excuse to leave," Sarah tearfully expressed.

"Fine," Alicia conceded, defeated. She sat back down, her displeasure evident. She despised the situation, but witnessing her mother's tears compelled her to stay. "What do you want to talk about?"

"For now, all we want is for you to tell us

what you would like as a birthday present. That's all," Damian stated.

"So, if I tell you what I want, you promise that's the only thing we'll discuss tonight?" Alicia asked, a smile playing on her lips. "If I come up with something that helps me uncover the truth about the man who killed Shantel, then I can finally be left alone. This could work to my advantage," she thought to herself.

"Yes," Damian replied, smiling. They were finally making headway with Alicia.

"Perfect. They have no idea what they've started by letting me choose what I want," Alicia mused. "In that case, I'd love to have a laptop." She retrieved a picture of the laptop she had set her sights on from her backpack. "I saw this one at the store the other day and took a picture of it. Do you think you can get this for me?"

Damian took the picture from Alicia and showed it to his wife. "I think this would be the perfect gift for her."

"You could use it for your school assignments," Sarah chimed in.

"Yes! That's exactly why I want it," Alicia lied. "If I have this, I won't need to rely on the school computers."

"Well, it's settled then. Tomorrow, after we

pick you up from school, we'll go to the store and get it for you," Damian confirmed.

Alicia opening up to her parents and expressing her desires alleviated the tension in the dining room, and her parents felt a glimmer of hope. Alicia, however, remained vigilant, ensuring that her parents had no intention of reneging on their promise to leave her alone, as long as she agreed to communicate with them when necessary. Finally, she would obtain the laptop she desperately needed to continue her research on Shantel's murder and inch closer to uncovering the identity of the killer and seeking her revenge.

"Mom? Dad?" Alicia forced a fake smile. "Now that we've had the conversation you wanted, and I've told you what I want, may I be excused?"

"Yes, of course," Sarah replied.

After Alicia left the dining room, Damian turned to his wife. "Well, that turned out better than I expected," he remarked.

"I suppose," Sarah said, taking a seat at the table. "Don't get me wrong. I'm glad she finally opened up to us and shared her desires, but I can't shake the feeling that there's more to it. What was with that sudden change in attitude?"

"That's all part of her depression, Sarah. Until she receives the help and medication from Dr. Barnes, we should anticipate these emotional ups and downs. Let's clean the dishes and go check on her. I'm sure you're worrying over nothing," Damian reassured his wife.

****

Sarah tossed and turned in bed that night, her mind plagued by unease. Something felt off about Alicia's recent behavior, and despite Damian's reassurances, she couldn't shake the nagging feeling. The dreams that haunted her that night only intensified her fears, morphing into vivid nightmares of Alicia's potential actions now that they had sought help from Dr. Barnes. The images of her daughter wielding a knife played over and over in her mind, leaving her restless and anxious.

Suddenly, Sarah's eyes fluttered open, her heart pounding. Sleep eluded her, and frustration settled in as she struggled to find tranquility. She tried to convince herself that it was all just her imagination running wild, that these were merely vivid dreams. But when she saw Alicia standing over her, a knife gleaming in her hand, Sarah's heart froze.

"Alicia?" Sarah's voice trembled with fear. "What are you doing?"

"I told you, my name is Shantel. Not Alicia!" Alicia retorted, her voice filled with anger and defiance.

"ALICIA! NO!" Sarah's scream pierced the air as she recoiled, terrified that her daughter was about to attack her. Her cries roused Damian from his sleep, his eyes widening at the sight of Alicia brandishing a knife.

"Alicia! What are you doing?" Damian's voice trembled with a mix of shock and concern.

"When are the two of you going to learn to call me by my real name? I won't ask again!" Alicia spat, her eyes brimming with anger. "MY NAME IS SHANTEL!"

Reacting swiftly, Damian lunged out of bed and rushed to Sarah's side, using his body as a shield between Alicia and her mother. "Alicia? Alicia?" he repeated, his voice desperate, hoping to break the hold of whatever trance had possessed her.

Alicia blinked, her eyes refocusing as she met her father's gaze. "Dad?" Her voice was calm, confusion evident in her tone. She glanced down at the knife in her hand. "What happened?"

"That's what we want to know," Damian replied, his voice filled with concern. "Your mother woke up and saw you standing over her with a knife."

Alicia's gaze shifted to Sarah, who sat trembling on the bed. "I don't remember coming in here. I don't know where I got the knife from." She looked back at her father. "I must've been sleepwalking again."

"What's the last thing you remember?" Damian asked, a trace of suspicion in his voice.

Alicia's mind raced, searching for a plausible explanation. She couldn't afford to be caught in the act of sneaking into their room. "I... I remember a nightmare. Yes, that's what it was. I was sleeping, and I had a nightmare. I didn't know what was going on. And the next thing I know, you're shaking me awake."

Relieved by Alicia's explanation, Damian gently took the knife from her hand. "Let me just take this from you," he said, his tone soothing. "And let's get you back into bed."

Alicia followed her father out of the room, casting a parting glare at her mother. She mouthed the words "Stop calling me Alicia" before retreating to her own room. Climbing back into bed, she watched as Damian tucked her in, her mind buzzing with plans for the future.

"Feeling better?" Damian asked, concern etched on his face.

"I am. Thank you, Dad," Alicia replied, feigning relief. "Can you tell Mom that I'm sorry about what happened tonight? Honestly, I didn't mean to scare her."

"I'll talk to her, but don't worry too much. I'm sure Mom understands that you were sleepwalking and didn't mean any harm. Now, get some sleep." Damian hugged Alicia tightly before returning to his own bedroom. "Well, I think she's finally calmed down for the night," he whispered to his wife.

Sarah, still visibly shaken, looked at Damian with a mix of fear and worry. "You can't tell me that this is normal behavior for a child, Damian," she pleaded, her voice quivering.

"Believe me, I don't find this normal at all," Damian admitted, his voice heavy with concern. "When we take her to Dr. Barnes next week, we'll make sure to inform her about this incident. Perhaps sleepwalking is part of the depression she's going through."

Tears welled up in Sarah's eyes as she voiced her deepest fear. "Damian, when you're at work during the week, I'm alone with her. What if she does something to me? I'm scared to be in my own home."

"I promise you, Sarah, I won't let her hurt you," Damian vowed, his voice filled with determination. He climbed into bed and pulled Sarah close, seeking to provide her with solace and reassurance. "Hopefully, Dr. Barnes will be able to prescribe the right medication to help Alicia. We'll get through this together."

Sarah clung to Damian, finding comfort in his words. She knew they had to trust in the expertise of the psychiatrist, hoping that the upcoming appointment would shed light on Alicia's troubling behavior and provide a path towards healing. As they lay there, holding each other tightly, their minds filled with worry and uncertainty, they both silently prayed for a resolution that would restore peace and harmony to their once-loving home.

∞ ∞ ∞

Chapter 19

Sarah's anxiety intensified as she anxiously awaited Alicia's next appointment with Doctor Barnes. The weight in her stomach seemed to grow heavier with each passing second she spent alone in the house with her daughter. Sarah's fear of what Alicia might do had reached a point where it consumed her thoughts entirely. Tuesday arrived sooner than she expected, and Sarah was relieved to finally have the opportunity to speak with the doctor and share the harrowing incident that had unfolded in their own bedroom.

"Doctor, could we speak with you before you talk to Alicia?" Sarah mustered the courage to request. She held a deep-seated suspicion that Alicia would fabricate stories or downplay the severity of the situation if given the chance to speak with the doctor first. Sarah needed to ensure that Doctor Barnes understood just how terrified she was to remain in the house with her own daughter.

"Of course, please come in," Doctor Barnes invited them into her office, their footsteps echoing softly against the floor as they entered. Sensing the urgency in their demeanor, the doctor guided them to their seats, her expression filled with concern. "Has there been any new developments since our last meeting?" she inquired gently, her voice poised and attentive.

Sarah took a deep breath, her words trembling as she struggled to recount the chilling encounter that had unfolded only a week prior. "You could say that," she began, her voice quivering with a mix of fear and distress. "Last week, I awoke to find Alicia standing over me with a knife. She claimed she was sleepwalking after having a nightmare, but deep down, I sensed that it was nothing more than a fabricated excuse. This was the second time I discovered her holding a knife in the dead of night, but this time, I genuinely believed she intended to harm me in my sleep. I'm consumed by fear within my own home, Doctor, and I despise living in this constant state of terror," Sarah revealed, her voice breaking as tears streamed down her face. The weight of her emotions becoming too overwhelming to contain any longer.

Turning to address Doctor Barnes, Damian interjected, his voice filled with a mixture of desperation and concern. "Doctor, during our last session, you mentioned the possibility of considering medication for Alicia due to her behavior. Is that still a viable option?" he asked, a flicker of hope lingering within his eyes.

Doctor Barnes regarded the couple gravely, her gaze filled with a somber understanding. "I believe we have surpassed the point where medication alone will suffice for Alicia's condition," she responded, her tone laced with a hint of regret. "Given what you've just shared with me, it appears that there may be a violent inclination within her that poses a significant threat to both of you. Moreover, there's a genuine concern that she may also inflict harm upon herself. This situation surpasses my area of expertise, and I suspect that Alicia's past experiences, particularly her treatment by her birth parents, might be playing a role in her current state."

Sarah's distress deepened, her voice trembling as she beseeched the doctor for guidance. "What do you suggest we do next? I can't bear the thought of being harmed by my own daughter simply because she didn't receive the help she so desperately needs," she implored, her vulnerability laid bare before Doctor Barnes.

Gently, yet resolutely, Doctor Barnes responded, her eyes conveying both empathy and a sense of duty. "The only viable course of action remaining is to admit Alicia to a mental health facility," she asserted, her voice imbued with a tone of inevitability. Aware of the overwhelming information being shared, the doctor reached into her desk and retrieved brochures, extending them to the couple with a sense of solemnity. "Take your time to review these options. These facilities are some of the best in the area and can provide the specific care and support that Alicia needs."

Damian briefly perused the brochures, his eyes scanning the words, before turning to Sarah, his voice resolute. "I believe this is the best course of action for Alicia," he affirmed, his conviction evident in his tone. Sarah nodded in agreement, her voice laden with a mix of determination and sorrow. "It seems that admitting her to a mental health facility is the only path forward. Thank you, Doctor Barnes. My husband and I will carefully review these brochures and promptly communicate our decision to you."

As they left the office, the weight of their emotions remained, but a glimmer of hope arose within Sarah and Damian. They were determined to find a solution for Alicia, one that would ensure her safety and well-being, even if it meant making the heart-wrenching decision to separate themselves from their daughter temporarily.

****

Alicia dashed into her bedroom as soon as

they arrived home from their meeting with Doctor Barnes. Normally, Sarah and Damian would have stopped her from running off, but the weight of the day's events hung heavily in the air, and the couple needed time alone to deliberate on what course of action to take concerning Alicia.

"Sarah, I understand that you despise the idea of sending her to a facility, but we have to prioritize what's best for her and for us," Damian said, placing the brochures down on the kitchen table, his voice tinged with a mixture of concern and determination.

"I wish it hadn't come to this, but you're right," Sarah sighed, her voice heavy with resignation. "She poses a danger to herself and to all of us if she remains here. But we waited so long to finally have a child, and now it feels like she's being taken away from us."

"We can't view it that way, Sarah. She isn't being taken away; she's going to a place where she'll receive the care and support she needs. It won't be forever—only until she's better and the doctors there can understand what she's going through," Damian reassured her, his voice filled with a mixture of compassion and hope.

"I know it's the right decision, but it still hurts," Sarah admitted, her voice laced with a mix of grief and guilt.

Unknown to her parents, Alicia had been descending the stairs and overheard fragments of their conversation. Curiosity mingled with anxiety as she wondered what her parents were discussing concerning her fate. She silently positioned herself behind the kitchen wall, her ears straining to catch every word that passed between them.

"So, we've come to a decision. She definitely needs to go to a mental health facility," Damian declared, his voice carrying a sense of finality. "Now, we have to choose which one. Doctor Barnes assured us that these places are exceptional, with programs specifically tailored to Alicia's needs."

Alicia's fists clenched involuntarily. She couldn't believe what she was hearing. Her parents were deliberating on sending her away. She pondered the reason behind their private conversation with Doctor Barnes earlier in the day, but the thought of betrayal never occurred to her. Suddenly, the doctor's persistent questions about the bedroom incident made sense—her parents were seeking evidence to support their decision.

"Damian, regardless of which facility we choose, let's make sure it's nearby so we can visit her regularly," Sarah suggested, her voice filled with a glimmer of hope.

Alicia's laughter erupted, bitter and devoid

of amusement. Her mother seemed to believe that everything would be fine as long as they visited her after they had shipped her off. Alicia was resolute - she wouldn't allow anyone to take her away. The notion of her parents willingly subjecting her to this fate felt like an unforgivable betrayal. They were well aware of her troubled past, of how she had been passed from one foster home to another after her biological parents abandoned her as a child. And now, they were repeating the cycle. But Alicia vowed that they would not get away with it.

Storming into her room, she flung her schoolbooks out of her backpack and began hastily packing clothes and other essentials she would need to survive on her own. "They think they can ship me off because they can't handle me? I don't need them. I never did," she muttered, her voice filled with defiance. "I already knew I was in this alone. And they believe they can send me away to someplace before I exact my vengeance on the murderer? That will never happen."

Alicia meticulously checked her backpack to ensure she had packed everything she would need for her escape. She surveyed her bedroom, searching for a way to leave the house undetected. The front door was out of the question since her parents would surely see her. Her gaze settled on the window, and a mix of anxiety and determination washed over her. She hesitated for a moment, contemplating the risks of climbing down from the second floor. But then, she noticed a tree conveniently positioned near her window. If she could navigate it carefully, she could climb out, jump onto the tree, and make her getaway.

Summoning her courage, Alicia maneuvered her way out of the window and onto the tree, inch by inch. She descended cautiously, her heart pounding in her chest. Once she reached the ground, she cast a final glance at the house she was leaving behind, knowing that she wouldn't miss living there. With renewed purpose, her thoughts shifted toward her quest to find Shantel's murderer.

Meanwhile, Damian and Sarah had reached a decision regarding Alicia's future but had agreed to consult with Doctor Barnes before discussing it with their daughter. Damian, understanding the importance of handling the situation delicately, suggested informing Alicia once they had guidance from the doctor.

"Let's wait until we've spoken to Doctor Barnes. We don't want Alicia to get upset with us for sending her away. The doctor will know the best way to approach this," Damian proposed, considering Alicia's emotional state.

"That's a wise idea. Please let her know that dinner will be ready soon," Sarah replied, acknowledging the need for caution. With that,

Damian proceeded upstairs to Alicia's room to deliver the message.

"Alicia? Please come down. Dinner will be ready soon," Damian called out, his voice echoing through the house. He waited, but there was no response from Alicia's room. Growing concerned, he called out again, only to be met with silence. Worried, he rushed upstairs to check on her.

"Sarah! Call the police!" Damian shouted, panic etched across his face, as he burst into their bedroom.

Sarah, bewildered by the urgency in Damian's voice, inquired anxiously, "What's happening? What did she do?"

"She's... she's not there," Damian stammered, struggling to find the right words to convey the gravity of the situation.

"What do you mean she's not there?" Sarah's confusion deepened. Neither of them had seen Alicia leave her room since they arrived home.

"Her room is empty, and the window is open. She must have climbed out," Damian explained, the realization dawning on him.

Sarah's hands trembled as she grabbed her phone, but her panic prevented her from dialing 911 effectively. Sensing her distress, Damian took the phone from her and made the call himself.

"Hello? This is Damian Atkinson. Our daughter is missing. When did it happen? It must have been within the last hour or so. She was in her room all this time, but when I went to get her for dinner, her room was empty, and the window was open. I don't think she was abducted; I have a feeling she may have climbed out. Our address? It's 4098 Hart Street. Yes, that's the house. Alright, I'll inform my wife. Thank you, officer," Damian relayed the details of Alicia's disappearance to the authorities.

Sarah, still in shock, pleaded for information, "What did they say?"

"At first, they were considering the standard waiting period of twenty-four hours, but when I mentioned our address and the history of this house, their approach changed. They want us to meet them at the local park, where an officer will speak with us," Damian explained, his voice laden with concern.

The couple hastily made their way to the park, unsure of what to expect but desperate for any information regarding their missing daughter. As they arrived, they were confronted by a group of police officers, a sight that caught them off guard.

"I wasn't expecting this," Damian muttered to himself, exiting the car and assisting Sarah out.

"Mr. and Mrs. Atkinson?" a police officer approached them. "I'm Officer Collins, and I'm in charge of this search party."

"Search party?" Damian questioned, surprised by the scale of the operation. "I wasn't aware there would be one. We were told an officer would meet and speak with us."

"In cases like these, we usually wait before organizing a search party, but given the history of your house, we didn't want to take any chances. Follow me; I have a few questions for both of you that will help us determine where to focus our search for your daughter," Officer Collins explained, his tone calm and reassuring.

Damian clasped Sarah's hand tightly as they followed Officer Collins. They provided a detailed account of Alicia's recent behavior and their attempts to seek professional help. Damian emphasized their discussion with Doctor Barnes regarding Alicia's potential placement in a mental health facility, which had been interrupted by Alicia's sudden disappearance.

"Sir, please don't worry. We will do everything within our power to locate your daughter," Officer Collins reassured the distraught parents, sensing their anxiety and fear.

∞ ∞ ∞

Chapter 20:

Sarah and Damian wasted no time in doing their part of the search, even though the cops already started. Officer Collins told them it would be best if they did their own searching, knowing more places where Alicia may have gone.

"Where should we go first?" Damian asked. It wasn't until this moment he realized how much he missed in his daughter's life by always being at work. He had no idea what places Alicia may have gone to.

"I...I don't know," Sarah couldn't think straight. "I don't know where she would've gone. She never goes anywhere besides school." She tried to think of the places where Alicia used to go with friends before she changed. "Wait. She used to hang out with Skye at the park near the school when we first moved here."

"Perfect. Let's put that on the list of places to check out. Officer Collins said we should start by checking the areas around our house since she hasn't been missing for long. Chances are, she may not have gotten far," Damian said.

"Good idea," Sarah agreed.

As they pressed forward with their determined search efforts, Sarah took on the task of reaching out to Alicia's relatives and parents of her classmates. Each call was a desperate plea for any inkling of information, any shred of hope that would bring them closer to finding the missing girl. The phone conversations were fraught with despair and anxiety, as one by one, the voices on the other end echoed the same disheartening response: they hadn't heard from Alicia.

Undeterred by the lack of leads, Sarah rallied the support of Alicia's extended family and the concerned parents, who all agreed to join forces with her and Damian in their quest to locate the young girl. Time was of the essence, and within the span of a mere half-hour, the search party began to take shape, swelling with the arrival of additional volunteers.

The group now comprised not only law enforcement officers, but a gathering of parents from Alicia's school who had abandoned their own worries to lend a helping hand. Alongside them stood the worried relatives of the Atkinson family, their faces etched with concern and determination. The atmosphere crackled with a mix of trepidation and resilience as this amalgamation of hearts and minds embarked on a unified mission.

Yet, for some among the search party, the sight of the assembled group triggered a haunting remembrance. Those who had resided in the neighborhood during the tragic days when Shantel's life was mercilessly taken felt an eerie sense of déjà vu. The memories of that fateful search party, their futile efforts to find Shantel alive, flooded their minds once more. The weight of the past hung heavy in the air, mingling with the raw emotions of the present.

But amid the haunting recollections, a flicker of hope ignited within each person's heart. Despite the grim echoes of the past, they clung to the belief that this time, the outcome would be different. Their collective resolve resonated through the streets, weaving a tapestry of determination and prayers, as they embarked on a search fueled by a desperate yearning for a happier ending.

"Where do you think we should search first?" Sarah asked her husband. The people broke up into groups to spread out and look for Alicia in different places.

"Do you know one place she enjoyed going besides her room?"

Sarah was quiet as she thought about it.

"The school! I bet that's where she went. Her teacher told me she spent recess alone in the playground. I wonder if she went there to be alone."

"Alright, let's start with going there and see if we can find any sign that she was there." Damian took his wife's hand and they walked to the school. The playground was dark and there wasn't a sign of Alicia there, diminishing the hope her parents felt before they arrived. "DAMN!" Damian yelled. He turned and saw his wife climbing through an opening in the fence. "Sarah, what are you doing? She isn't here."

"I know that, but what if she was here? Look, I don't want to take any chances. What if she left a clue? Are you forgetting what happened to the girl who lived in our house? She was kidnapped. What if..." she couldn't finish her sentence and started to cry.

Damian climbed through the fence and wrapped his arms around Sarah. "I know it's hard to not think the worst, but we have to. I'm sure Alicia wasn't kidnapped and she just ran off. We know she has something wrong and can't think clearly. But if it'll make you feel better, we'll check the schoolyard and then we'll be off to the next location."

After finding no signs that Alicia was ever at the schoolyard, they searched the area around the school, only to come up empty-handed. The couple asked people who lived in the area and no one had seen Alicia. Sarah and Damian were running out of options.

"Where do we look now?" Damian asked.

"Red Fern Garden," Sarah replied.

"Red Fermn what?"

"It's a park I drive past when I pick Alicia up from school. I never took notice of it before, but the other day when I was driving her home, she mentioned to me how beautiful the park looked from the car window. I thought it was odd when she brought it up because she hardly talked to me in the car. I can't believe I forgot about the park until now."

"Well, what are we waiting for? Let's get back to the car and drive over to the park."

Sarah knew she shouldn't have gotten her hopes up as Damian drove to the park, but she couldn't help it. Something inside of her told her that this time, the outcome would be different. She jumped out of the car when Damian pulled up to the park and started to scream for her daughter.

"ALICIA! ALICIA! ARE YOU HERE?"

Damian's heart broke, watching his wife standing in the middle of the park, screaming for their daughter. There wasn't a soul in the park except for the two of them. They were wasting their time being here.

"Sarah, come," Damian called urgently, his grip tightening around his wife's trembling hand. The tears that streamed down Sarah's face were abruptly interrupted as she turned her attention to her husband's words. "She's not here. There is one other place I think we should try, though."

Her voice quivering with a mix of hope and confusion, Sarah sought clarification. "Where?" She wiped away the remnants of her tears, desperately searching for a glimmer of solace.

Damian's gaze held a flicker of determination as he uttered the words that pierced through the haze of uncertainty. "Cathedral of Purpose."

The mention of their old church sent ripples of confusion through Sarah's mind. Memories of a bygone era resurfaced, fragments of a time when hope still danced in their hearts. Cathedral of Purpose had been their sanctuary, a spiritual refuge they had frequented in the early days of their life in the neighborhood. But as their struggles with Alicia had escalated, their visits dwindled, eventually ceasing altogether. "Our old church?" Sarah's voice carried a mix of disbelief and curiosity. "Why do you think she'd be there?"

A fleeting vulnerability passed over Damian's face, mingling with the fatigue etched into his features. "I'm running out of ideas, and that's the last place I can think of."

Sarah's own well of ideas had run dry, the reservoir of possibilities now barren. Doubt gnawed at her, but she clung to the flickering embers of hope. With a resolve born from desperation, she nodded in agreement. She couldn't fathom the likelihood of finding Alicia within the hallowed walls of the church, but the mere act of searching there felt like a lifeline of sorts.

Their car's tires whispered against the asphalt as they navigated the familiar streets, leading them to the Cathedral of Purpose. The grandeur of the church loomed before them, its majestic spires reaching toward the heavens. The sun cast intricate patterns of light and shadow upon the timeless stone facade, imbuing the structure with an ethereal glow.

Sarah and Damian stepped out of their vehicle, their footsteps echoing in the quietude that enveloped the sacred grounds. As they crossed the threshold into the sanctuary, a hushed reverence settled upon them. The air was heavy with the fragrance of frankincense and aged wood, an olfactory tapestry that wove itself into their memories.

Silent prayers whispered upon their lips as they explored every nook and cranny, their eyes scouring the pews and alcoves for any sign of their beloved daughter. But the church remained cloaked in an eerie stillness, its vast expanse echoing their unanswered calls. Alicia's absence was palpable, and a profound sense of emptiness settled upon their hearts.

With a heavy sigh, Sarah retreated from the nave, her hand instinctively reaching for the door that separated the sacred space from the outside world. The resounding thud of her car door echoed through the air, a testament to the weight of their disappointment and the unyielding grip of their anguish.

"Now what do we do?" Sarah turned to Damian.

"There's nothing else for us to do but go back to the park and let Officer Collins know we didn't have luck finding her."

Officer Collins was waiting for the couple when they returned to the park. One look at the parents' faces and she knew they had no luck finding the girl.

"Please tell me you had better luck than the two of us," Damian asked the officer.

"I really am sorry, but my men are still

searching. Plus, the search teams are still out there. I think the best thing for the two of you to do is to go home. It's getting dark," Officer Collins said.

"How are we supposed to go home when our daughter is still missing?" Sarah cried.

"Sweetie," Damian tried to calm his wife. "Officer Collins is right. We're not going to be much help with the search. We're far too emotional to think straight and it is getting late. Let's go home and we can come up with a plan for tomorrow."

*****

The kitchen was dimly lit, with a single overhead light casting a soft glow that barely reached the corners of the room. The air was heavy, filled with anticipation and worry, as Sarah and Damian anxiously awaited any news about Alicia. The ticking of the old wall clock seemed to echo through the silence, intensifying the feeling of time slipping away.

Sarah sat at the worn wooden table, her fingers nervously tapping against its surface. Her hazel eyes were fixed on the phone, willing it to ring, her mind consumed with thoughts of Alicia's safety. The weight of the situation pressed heavily on her shoulders, causing her chest to tighten with each passing minute.

Damian leaned against the kitchen counter. His face was etched with concern, lines of worry etched deeply into his forehead. He absentmindedly ran a hand through his disheveled hair, his normally composed demeanor shattered by Alicia's disappearance. He had insisted that Sarah stay put, fearing that her involvement would only complicate matters. Despite his own apprehension, he tried to maintain a sense of calm for Sarah's sake.

Outside, the fading light of the day cast long shadows that danced across the kitchen window. The last remnants of sunlight painted the sky in hues of orange and pink, slowly giving way to the encroaching darkness. The distant sounds of crickets and the occasional passing car filtered through the stillness, a stark contrast to the turmoil inside the kitchen.

A sense of helplessness hung in the air, mingling with the scent of freshly brewed coffee and the faint aroma of dinner that lingered from earlier. The walls, adorned with family photographs and a colorful calendar, seemed to close in on Sarah and Damian, trapping them in their shared worry. The room felt both suffocating and empty, as if the absence of Alicia's presence left a void that nothing could fill.

As the minutes turned into hours, the tension in the kitchen grew thicker, each passing moment amplifying the gravity of the situation. Every ring of the telephone, every creak of the floorboards, sent their hearts racing, only to be followed by a crushing disappointment as the calls turned out to be unrelated to Alicia's disappearance.

In that moment, the kitchen became a microcosm of their emotions, a space where hope, fear, and uncertainty converged. The weight of the unknown hung heavily in the air, suffusing the room with an almost tangible anxiety. Sarah and Damian sat in the kitchen, bound by their shared desperation, their world narrowed to the confines of that dimly lit space, waiting for a call that would bring them closer to finding Alicia and restoring a semblance of normalcy to their shattered lives.

The front door opened and Alicia stepped into the living room. "Mom? Dad? Are you home?"

Sarah looked up at her husband when she heard Alicia's voice. "Great, now I'm losing my mind. I swear I heard her come into the house."

"Mom? Dad?" Alicia called out to them again.

"She's back!" Sarah jumped up from her chair. "She's back!" They rushed into the living room and saw Alicia standing in the doorway. "Alicia?"

"Mom!" Alicia threw her backpack on the floor and ran to her parents. "Mom! Dad" She couldn't control her sobbing as Sarah and Damian pulled her into a tight hug.

"Sweetie, we've been so worried about you," Sarah cried on Alicia's head. "Where did you go?"

"I...I don't remember."

Sarah and Damian looked at each other, wondering if they could believe what she said. She used the excuse of sleepwalking before, but this was serious. She left the house and couldn't be found.

"What matters is you're here now and safe," Damian said. He pulled away to look at his daughter, tears streaming down Alicia's face. "Are you alright? Were you hurt?"

Alicia continued to cry. "I don't think so. I feel fine. Honestly."

"I think what we all need right now is to calm down," Damian said. "Alicia, why don't you go upstairs to your room and get cleaned up. And keep your bedroom door open," he said, afraid she would try to run off again.

"Do you think she's telling us the truth?" Sarah asked once Alicia was upstairs.

"Hard to tell with her," Damian sighed. "But

she's back home and that's what matters."

"Speaking of that, I better call Officer Collins up and let her know Alicia is here." Sarah grabbed her phone and called the number the officer gave her before they left the park.

"Office Collins," she answered.

"Officer, this is Sarah Atkinson. Alicia just showed up at home."

"She did? That's wonderful news. Do you know where she was?"

"That's the only problem. We asked her where she was, but she says she doesn't remember. But she said she was fine and wasn't hurt. She's in her room right now, but we're going to keep an eye on her to make sure she doesn't sneak out again."

"I'm so glad to hear she's home. This could've turned out a lot worse. Trust me, I've seen cases where the children never come home. I'm glad that wasn't the case with Alicia," Officer Collins said.

"Damian and I can't thank you and your team for all the help. Oh wait, I just remembered, that the search for Alicia is still going on. I don't know who to call to tell them she came home," Sarah stressed.

"You've got enough on your hands, I don't

want you to think about that. I'll take care of it. I'll call my team and they'll pass the word around to your neighbors and relatives that the search is over."

"Thank you so much, officer. That takes a lot of stress off of us. I'll let my husband know. Again, thank you."

"What did she say?" Damian asked when Sarah ended the phone call.

"She's happy to hear Alicia is back. She also said for us not to worry about the search party. She'll contact them and tell them the great news." Sarah let out a deep sigh and sat at the kitchen table. "I don't know what to make out of what happened today."

"Neither do I. But it's over and we have to look towards the future now and get Alicia the help she needs."

∞ ∞ ∞

Chapter 21:

The morning sunlight streamed through the kitchen window, casting a warm glow that illuminated the room. The worn, wooden table stood as a centerpiece, graced with a simple breakfast spread. The tantalizing aroma of sizzling bacon and freshly flipped pancakes wafted through the air, awakening the senses and beckoning the family to gather.

As Sarah stood by the stove, her movements were slow and deliberate, the fatigue from the sleepless night evident in the lines that etched her face. Her tired eyes flickered with a glimmer of hope as she watched the golden pancakes take shape, their edges turning a delightful shade of caramel brown. The comforting sizzle of bacon filled the kitchen, creating a symphony of sounds that provided a semblance of normalcy amidst the recent chaos.

Damian sat at the table, his attention momentarily diverted from the newspaper that lay before him. He folded it gently, setting it aside as Alicia entered the room. Her presence brought a newfound tranquility to the space, her youthful energy laced with a touch of curiosity. The morning light danced in her eyes, reflecting a renewed sense of calm after a tumultuous night.

Alicia approached the table, her steps tentative yet purposeful. As she took her seat, the worn chair creaked softly, serving as a reminder of the unspoken tension that had plagued the household. Damian's gaze lingered on her, his concern melting into relief at the sight of her safe return.

"How are you feeling this morning?" Damian's voice carried a mix of paternal concern and genuine care, his words a lifeline reaching out to his daughter.

Alicia's smile radiated warmth, a flicker of gratitude shining through her eyes. "Much better than I have been," she responded, her voice carrying a sense of newfound strength. "Thank you for asking. I still don't know what happened yesterday."

Sarah approached the table, a plate laden with fluffy pancakes and crispy bacon in hand. She set it down before Alicia, a tangible gesture of love and comfort. Her touch conveyed a silent reassurance that they were there for her, ready to support and protect her in whatever way they could.

"Don't worry about that, sweetie," Sarah's voice held a soothing tone, her eyes filled with maternal tenderness. "It's all in the past. Today is a fresh start."

Damian's gaze shifted between Sarah and Alicia, his concern intertwining with a glimmer of optimism. The events of the previous day still lingered in the air, their impact palpable, but the resilience of his daughter tugged at his heartstrings.

"Given what happened last night, do you want to stay home today?" Damian's question carried a note of caution, a gentle reminder of the dangers that lurked beyond the safety of their home.

Alicia's eyes sparkled with determination, a newfound resolve shining through. She paused for a moment, savoring the aroma of the breakfast before her. The weight of her decision hung in the air, the room holding its breath as her response took shape.

"Actually, I think I want to go to school," Alicia's voice held a hint of excitement, her words breaking the silence. "I want to see my friends."

Sarah and Damian exchanged glances, their eyes mirroring a mixture of surprise and joy. The mention of friends, a glimmer of social connection, was a welcome change from the isolation that had enveloped Alicia for months. Despite the previous day's harrowing events, Alicia's desire to return to her routine, to seek solace in the company of her peers, was a testament to her resilience.

A sense of unspoken agreement settled over the room. Sarah reached out and gently squeezed Alicia's hand, a silent affirmation of support. Damian's smile, tinged with a touch of apprehension, spoke volumes about the protective love he harbored for his daughter. They were ready to let her spread her wings once more, to navigate the world outside their cocoon with newfound strength and determination.

"As long as you feel you're up to it, I don't see it being a problem," Damian said.

"I do. As I said yesterday, I don't know what happened or how I ended up outside. I was hoping to remember where I went yesterday, but I still have no idea."

"Well, we don't want you to think about that anymore. We're glad to have our daughter back," Sarah smiled. She didn't know what happened since Alicia ran away, but the girl sitting at the table wasn't the one they were having problems with for the past few months. The girl she saw now was the cheerful girl she and Damian knew and loved.

"Why are you looking at me? Am I in trouble?" Alicia asked, seeing her parents watch her eat.

"No. You're not in trouble at all. We're just so glad to have you back," Sarah said, choking back tears.

"What your mother means is we haven't seen you this happy in months. And we're glad to see that smile of yours again."

Alicia looked weirdly at her parents. "What are you talking about?"

"Well, I don't know how to put this, but you haven't been this happy in a long time," Sarah said. "There's a change in you. A good one. You've gone back to being the girl who came to live with us a year ago. And we're so happy."

"Okay," Alicia raised an eyebrow. "I don't know what you're talking about. I've always been the same girl."

Damian turned to Sarah and shrugged before bringing his attention back to Alicia. "Sweetie, do you have any memory of what happened before yesterday?"

Alicia shook her head. "I remember us living in the city until you decided to move here. And starting school here. Oh, and my friend Skye.

Do you know why I haven't heard from her in a while?"

"Sweetie, Skye stopped coming over because you kept saying you didn't want to hang out with her," Sarah said.

"I did?" Alicia was confused. "Why would I do that? I loved playing with her."

"We know you did and that's why we found it odd when you didn't want to hang out with her. Emily and Sophia also came over to hang out with you, but you said no. You really don't remember wanting to stay alone in your room?" Damian said.

"Mom? Dad? I don't remember much of anything that's happened," Alicia said.

"You know what? Let's not talk about this anymore," Sarah said. She was getting scared at how Alicia had no memory of what happened and was afraid she would let it slip about Alicia thinking her name was Shantel. "Alicia, if you want to make it to school in time, you need to get ready."

"You're right. I'm running late," Alicia said, throwing her plates in the sink and rushing upstairs to get ready for school.

"Well, that certainly is weird," Damian said. "I can't believe she has no recollection of what's been going on."

****

The school's campus stretched out before them, a sprawling expanse of neatly manicured lawns, towering trees, and red-brick buildings. The morning sun cast a golden hue across the scene, illuminating the vibrant colors of autumn leaves that rustled in the gentle breeze. It was a picturesque setting, one that belied the tumultuous events that had unfolded just hours before.

As Damian parked the car in the school's designated drop-off zone, the engine's rumble faded into the background, replaced by the sounds of youthful chatter and the distant ringing of the school bell. The air was charged with a palpable energy, the anticipation of a new day mingled with the lingering remnants of the previous night's ordeal.

Alicia stepped out of the car, her backpack slung over one shoulder, her movements a delicate balance of uncertainty and determination. The familiar sights and sounds of the schoolyard enveloped her, a cacophony of laughter, conversations, and hurried footsteps. The vibrant chatter of her peers filled the air, a symphony of adolescence echoing through the corridors of academia.

Damian and Sarah walked alongside Alicia,

their protective instincts heightened as they navigated the bustling campus. The school building loomed before them, its imposing presence softened by the warm morning light that filtered through the windows. The scent of freshly polished floors mingled with the faint aroma of books, a heady mix of academia and possibility.

They made their way to the principal's office, its door adorned with a small brass plaque that read "Principal Avil." The room itself exuded an air of authority, with bookshelves lining the walls, filled to the brim with volumes on education, leadership, and child psychology. The desk, meticulously organized, stood as a focal point, the embodiment of a figurehead whose responsibility extended to the welfare of every student under their care.

Principal Avil greeted them with a warm smile, his demeanor a blend of professionalism and empathy. His office, bathed in natural light streaming through the windows, felt like a sanctuary, a space where concerns could be shared and resolutions found. The walls, adorned with diplomas and framed motivational quotes, served as a testament to his dedication and the transformative power of education.

Damian and Sarah sat opposite the principal, their faces etched with a mixture of exhaustion and concern. The weight of the previous night's events still lingered, casting a shadow over their expressions. They recounted the events, their voices carrying a sense of urgency and vulnerability. Every word was carefully chosen, their desire to protect Alicia palpable in their every syllable.

Principal Avil listened attentively, his gaze unwavering, his presence a calming force in the storm of their emotions. He nodded, his understanding evident, as he assured them that he would take every precaution to ensure Alicia's well-being. His commitment to the safety and welfare of his students was unwavering, a resolute dedication that shone through his words.

"I will personally keep an eye on Alicia," Principal Avil stated, his voice laced with reassurance. "I'll ensure she is surrounded by supportive peers and trusted faculty members. If anything happens, rest assured, we will contact you immediately."

A sigh of relief escaped Sarah's lips, her tension visibly easing. A fleeting glimpse of hope flickered in Damian's eyes, mingled with gratitude for the principal's understanding and commitment. In that moment, they knew that Alicia would be in good hands, cocooned within the protective embrace of a school community that cared deeply for its students.

As they left the principal's office, the weight

on their shoulders felt lighter, replaced by a renewed sense of trust and optimism. The school's hallways stretched out before them, a labyrinth of lockers, classrooms, and shared spaces teeming with the vibrancy of youth. Alicia walked alongside her parents, her steps a little lighter, her gaze fixed on the possibilities that lay ahead.

And so, as they bid farewell to the principal, their footsteps echoing through the hallway, they understood that within the confines of these school walls, Alicia would find both sanctuary and growth. The campus, pulsating with the promise of knowledge and connections, would serve as a guiding light, illuminating her path towards healing and rediscovery.

"Don't you have to get to the dealership?" Sarah asked when they returned home later that morning.

"After all we've been through since last night, I thought it would be best if I stayed home with you. Plus, we don't know what might happen with Alicia. I don't want you going through that alone." Damian sat on the couch and turned on the television.

The living room enveloped them in a serene ambiance, its walls adorned with cherished family photographs and shelves lined with well-worn books. The soft glow of the lamp cast a warm, intimate light, dancing across the room and casting gentle shadows on the plush furniture that cradled them. It was a haven of comfort, a sanctuary where they sought solace from the trials that had befallen their lives.

As Sarah removed her coat and placed her purse aside, the weight of the day's events lifted momentarily, allowing her to fully immerse herself in the haven of their living room. She approached the couch where Damian sat, his presence a magnetic force drawing her near. With a tender grace, she settled herself beside him, her body nestling into the contours of his embrace.

Sarah's head found its resting place on Damian's strong shoulder, the touch of his warm skin against her temple a balm to her weary soul. The familiar scent of his cologne mingled with the comforting aroma of the room, creating a sensory symphony that enveloped her senses. The gentle rise and fall of Damian's chest, synchronized with her own, offered a rhythm of security and stability.

In this tender moment, Sarah relished the physical closeness they shared, a reminder of the bond that had carried them through both joyous and challenging times. She longed for this intimacy, the simple act of being close, which had become a rarity in the wake of their recent trials. The comfort of his arms wrapped protectively around her provided a respite from the uncertainties that had clouded their lives.

As Damian's arm encircled her, drawing her nearer, his touch became a lifeline of connection. He pressed a gentle kiss atop her head, a tender gesture that conveyed both love and reassurance. The words that followed, "I love you," carried a weight that transcended the confines of the room, reaching deep into the recesses of Sarah's heart.

Her eyes fluttered closed, blocking out the outside world as she surrendered to the moment, allowing the love and tenderness to wash over her. Yet, amidst the warmth and affection, there was an unspoken question lingering in the air, a quiet uncertainty that cast a faint shadow over the tranquility they had found.

As Sarah held onto Damian's embrace, her mind wrestled with the unspoken thoughts that tugged at her consciousness. The fear of a potential separation, once voiced and now seemingly dormant, still lingered in the recesses of her thoughts. She yearned for the reassurance that their love would prevail, that the trials they had faced would not tear them apart.

In the hushed stillness of the room, Sarah mustered the courage to address the unspoken worry that gnawed at her soul. She took a deep breath, feeling the rise and fall of Damian's chest beneath her cheek, a reminder of the steadiness he offered.

"I love you too," she whispered, her voice a delicate thread woven with vulnerability. Her words hung in the air, pregnant with unspoken meaning. It was a declaration, a testament to the depth of her love, but also a plea for reassurance in the face of an uncertain future.

In that moment, their embrace held not just physical closeness, but the weight of unspoken conversations, the desire for open communication, and a shared hope for a future that defied the odds. As they nestled against each other, basking in the warmth of their togetherness, they knew that their journey was far from over, and that the path ahead would require unwavering love, understanding, and a willingness to confront the shadows that threatened to consume them.

"What's on your mind?" Damian asked.

"I was thinking… never mind. It's stupid," she shook her head.

"Sarah, after everything we've been through, there's nothing stupid about what's going on in your mind. You know you can tell me anything," he turned and looked into his wife's eyes.

Here it goes, she took a deep breath. "Damian, do you think we've gotten past our issues?"

"Is that what you were afraid to ask me?" He smiled. "I think now is the perfect time to discuss that."

"You do?" Sarah asked. She was afraid Damian was going to be upset at her for bringing up something he mentioned that seemed like ages ago.

"It's been on my mind, too. Especially the way Alicia came home, acting as if nothing happened last night. I was thinking about it all last night. And I think I've come to a conclusion. I think all this was a case of Alicia going through a weird phase."

"Alicia?" Sarah didn't know why he was talking about their daughter. That wasn't what was bothering her, though she was still confused by the sudden change in her daughter.

"Yes. You asked if I thought we were finished with her issues. And I think we are. I know what you're going to say, that Doctor Barnes suggested sending her to a mental health facility, but I don't think we have to anymore. You saw how she was this morning. She's back to being the girl we adopted. What I think is that she was acting like your typical pre-teen. Don't you remember what it was like to be eleven? I'm sure we didn't know what we were doing most of the time back then."

"Damian, that's not what I was talking about. Yes, I do agree there was quite a change in Alicia, we'll have to wait and see what happens with her. We don't know if she'll snap again. But what I was talking about was us," Sarah admitted.

"What about us?"

"Damian, don't you remember when this all began with Alicia, you brought up the idea of us getting separated."

And there it was. Damian wondered when his wife was going to bring this up again. He was speaking out of frustration that day and had no intentions of leaving his wife. They didn't know what was going on with Alicia at that point, not that they had answers now, but he wouldn't leave Sarah to raise Alicia on her own.

"I have regretted saying that to you since that night," Damian looked down. "That was during one of the nights neither of us knew what we were saying to one another. Truth is, I will never leave you, Sarah. You're right. We don't know if Alicia will snap again and that is why we need to stick together, so we can help Alicia and be a family."

Sarah smiled and wrapped her arms around Damian. "You have no idea how happy it makes me hear you say this. That's what has been worrying me all this time. What if you decided we should separate and I was left alone to raise Alicia? I know you said you didn't mean what you said that day, but it burned in the back of my mind that it was suggested."

"And that is why we should never keep secrets from each other," he held Sarah's body close to his. "I think we'll have to work a little on getting our marriage back to the way it was before Alicia came to live with us, but I have faith that we can do it."

"I do, too," Sarah reached up and kissed her husband. "And who knows? You might be right about Alicia going through a phase. Look at how she was this morning. She doesn't remember anything that happened."

"Maybe she shouldn't remember," Damian said. "And I think it would be best if we don't talk about it around her anymore. We don't want to take any chances that might trigger her."

"Good idea," Sarah agreed. "Guess all we can do is take it one day at a time."

"That's the best thing for us to do." Damian leaned down and kissed his wife. "I love you."

"I love you too." Sarah closed her eyes and cuddled up against her husband. After this discussion, she felt more at ease knowing that her marriage wasn't in danger. Together, the two could overcome anything. The past few months proved that with what happened with Alicia. She hoped that this was the beginning of the three of them becoming a happy family, the one she always wanted.

$\infty \infty \infty$

Chapter 22:

The ray of morning sun penetrated the windows, bathing the living room in a warm, golden light. The room seemed to exhale a collective sigh of relief, its walls witnessing the gradual restoration of tranquility and normalcy. Sarah stood in the center of the room, her eyes surveying the familiar surroundings that had become a sanctuary once more.

The stillness of the house enveloped her, broken only by the distant hum of everyday life outside its walls. With Alicia at school and Damian engrossed in his work, a rare solitude embraced Sarah, allowing her thoughts to wander through the labyrinth of recent memories. It was hard to fathom that mere weeks ago, her home had been fraught with tension and unease, a constant state of vigilance overshadowing even the simplest of tasks.

Taking a deep breath, Sarah closed her eyes and let the air fill her lungs, relishing the newfound sense of freedom that coursed through her veins. The weight of worry and apprehension that had burdened her for so long seemed to dissipate, replaced by a renewed energy and a glimmer of hope. It was as if the air itself whispered promises of a brighter future, where their lives could once again find stability and joy.

With the laundry bell chiming in the background, Sarah descended the stairs, her steps light and purposeful. The sound of the washing machine drumming to a halt heralded the completion of yet another mundane household task. As she entered the laundry room, the scent of clean linen mingled with the warmth of the dryer's exhaust, creating a comforting embrace of domesticity.

Sarah's hands grasped the laundry basket, its weight a tangible reminder of the everyday routines that now held a newfound significance. As she ascended the stairs, her footsteps whispered against the carpeted steps, leading her to Alicia's room. The door stood ajar, an invitation to a space that had once been a source of anxiety and uncertainty.

With a gentle push, Sarah entered the room, her eyes scanning the familiar surroundings. The walls, adorned with posters of Alicia's favorite bands and artwork, breathed life into the space, reflecting the tastes and aspirations of a young girl on the cusp of adolescence. The bed, neatly made, stood as a symbol of restful nights and peaceful dreams, its pillows fluffed and inviting.

A sense of calm washed over Sarah as she took in the sight before her. Alicia's room was no longer a battlefield of rebellion and chaos, but a haven of innocence and growth. The scattered toys now found their place on shelves, the clothes neatly folded and put away, a testament to a daughter who had emerged from the darkness and rediscovered her own light.

A smile tugged at the corners of Sarah's lips, a mixture of relief and gratitude. The room felt alive, vibrant with the essence of a young girl whose spirit had been rekindled. It was a visual testament to the resilience of their family, the triumph over adversity, and the unyielding power of love.

As Sarah turned to leave, the weight of the laundry basket in her hands felt lighter, its contents a symbol of the restored harmony that permeated their lives. With each step she took, ascending the stairs back towards the realm of the ordinary, Sarah carried with her a renewed sense of hope. The room behind her stood as a reminder that their journey was far from over, but the path ahead was paved with the promise of a future filled with happiness, growth, and the unwavering bond of a family that had weathered the storm together.

Downstairs, the television was on. Sarah

did her chores best when there was noise in the house. One of her favorite comedies was on this morning and she was laughing along with the funny lines as she put away Alicia's clothes. There were moments when she wanted to search through the dresser drawers, but she reminded herself that there was nothing wrong with Alicia. She was back to being her old self and wasn't hiding anything.

Sarah laughed at how silly she was acting. Two weeks ago, she and Damian decided they would trust Alicia, slowly, but so far, she hadn't shown them any signs that she was retreating back to how she was months ago.

"We interrupt this broadcast for breaking news," the news anchor's voice came across the television. Sarah stopped what she was doing to listen to the news. "We're on the scene in Mobile, Alabama where the body was found. Our very own anchor, Mark Hill, is on the scene."

"Thank you," Mark said. "The body of Anthony Welch was found in Fletcher Plaza early this morning. We are being told by the investigators here that he's been dead for at least a couple of weeks. The name of the victim may sound familiar to the people of Mobile. Anthony Welch was named the suspect in the murder of Shantel Thompson fifty years ago. Due to lack of evidence, he wasn't charged. The verdict left many of the residents furious and fearful that a murderer was loose on the streets. The family of Shantel didn't take the news well and moved out of their home not long after the trial."

"Mark, has there been any word on how he was killed?" The anchor asked.

"Yes. They found multiple stab wounds on his body. Unfortunately, there aren't any leads. The investigators will let us know once they have more information. Given the history of the victim, it has raised many questions as to who would've done this to the man. Was it one of Shantel's family members? A resident who feared what this man might do to other children? Whoever committed his crime, it definitely is going to open up a lot of wounds from what happened all those years ago. As soon as we get more information, we will let you know. Back to you at the studio," Mark said.

"This certainly wasn't the kind of news we were expecting this morning," the anchor said. "For those who don't know the story of Shantel Thompson and her murder, let us refresh your memory."

Sarah stopped what she was doing and rushed downstairs to catch the news program. She and Damian already did research on the murder of Shantel, but she hoped this would answer more questions.

"Shantel Thompson was only ten when she was kidnapped from in front of her house," the anchor said as a photo of Shantel flashed across the screen. "She was the adopted daughter of Gary and Sharon Riggs. The family did all they could to catch the murderer. They were hopeful when Anthony Welch was caught. However, that hope diminished when the court let the suspect go due to a lack of evidence. The distress was too overwhelming, they left Mobile and weren't heard from again."

Sarah couldn't listen to the news for another second. Everything that she'd been through with her daughter over the past few months was coming back. She went back upstairs to Alicia's room to continue putting the clothes away, but she couldn't shake the news from her head. *What are the odds that the suspect in Shantel's murder would be found dead after all these years? And after everything we've been through since moving here?* She thought. *Oh well. It's in the past. I don't even know why I'm thinking about it,* she laughed and went over to Alicia's closet to hang up her clothes.

The closest wasn't as organized as the rest of Alicia's room and it looked as if she just threw everything in there. *Guess I'm adding cleaning out the closet to my list of things to do,* she made a mental note.

That was going to be a project for another day, knowing it was going to take all day to clean out the closet. She continued to put away Alicia's clothes when she found an old backpack hidden in the back of the closet. *Hmm, I don't remember buying this for her.* She pulled it out from the boxes it was under and was surprised to see there were items inside. *What on earth are you hiding in here, Alicia?* She could feel her heart pound as she tried to figure out what to do next.

Part of her wanted to open the bag and find what her daughter was hiding from her and her husband. Then again, did she really want to know? Alicia was finally trusting them again and if she found out Sarah was snooping through her things, she wouldn't be happy. Still, there was this feeling that there was more to this backpack and Sarah had to get to the bottom of it.

Sarah, you're thinking too much into this than you have to. I bet it's nothing in here but dirty laundry Alicia forgot about, she laughed at the thought. *That would be funny, wouldn't it? Being afraid to open the bag up, only to find dirty laundry.* She was confused as to how Alicia got this backpack in the first place. It didn't look like one she bought her, nor did it look like any she'd seen in the stores. But it had to be Alicia's. How else would it get inside her closet?

She brought the backpack over to Alicia's

bed and sat down, not knowing what to expect when she opened it. Inside were piles of clothes. *Just as I thought, dirty clothes,* Sarah laughed. *That isn't anything bad.* Pulling the clothes out of the bag, she noticed bloodstains. At first, she didn't think anything of it. Alicia was a child and children fell a lot when they were outside playing. *I bet she was afraid of me seeing that she got blood on them.*

Sarah put the clothes aside to throw into the laundry once she was finished in there. She was about to put the bag back in the closet when she felt something sharp in the bottom of the bag. Carefully, she pulled the item out and found a knife covered in blood. *How in the world did this get in here?*

Her hands were shaking as she placed the knife down on the bed. *What am I supposed to do now?* She couldn't think straight. Sarah closed her eyes and tried to catch her breath. *Think Sarah. Think.*

After a few minutes, Sarah was able to clear her mind and she remembered the news she heard. *Wait a second! Shantel Thompson. Shantel!* She couldn't believe how she forgot about Alicia saying her name is Shantel.

No. No. No. Her mind started to race. This couldn't be happening. Was her daughter possessed by the ghost of this girl? She didn't know if she should call Damian and tell him what she discovered. He would think this was a case of her imagination running wild due to how many crime shows she watches. But she wasn't imagining this knife. She looked down at it next to her on the bed. *There has got to be more to do this.*

Sarah always believed in ghosts and spirits, especially those who had unfinished business here on earth, but she never thought she would experience something like this in her life. There were too many similarities between Alicia and Shantel, starting with the fact that both were adopted after they were abandoned by their birth parents. Added to that fact, both were ten years old when they lived in this house. And then there was the time Alicia only answered to the name Shantel. Sarah wondered if her daughter, or was it really Shantel, who was involved with the murder of this man.

About The Author

Curtis Maynard

 Curtis Maynard is an independent filmmaker, screenwriter, and author passionate about suspenseful storytelling. Enthralled by the paranormal, his mysteries and thrillers feature everything from hauntings and visions to cryptic messages from beyond the grave. Curtis currently resides with his wife and son in Alabama, a setting rich with inspiration for his novels and short films. He hopes his stories will leave you spellbound, disquieted, and suspicious of the slightest shuddering shadow.

Your review of this book is greatly appreciated!